Life Hack

Life Hack

A Migrant's Romance Book 1: Colombia

Ana Dantra

Dedication

To that Colombian girl I met so many years back in the Sawgrass mall. Your story is very different from this, but you planted the seed for it. I forgot your name, but I'll never forget *you*.

Acknowledgments

This book took five years in the making, and many people added ideas or constraints that changed it several times. Three people though I feel have contributed the most. Kathryn, who patiently read and edited the twenty versions that lead to this final manuscript. Miika, who said a novella wasn't enough, which forced me to have a deep talk with my characters and, in the process, understand there was a saga in the making. Russel, who believed in these books, took the time to really know the characters and added changes that helped them express a lot better.

Chapter 1

Hack

Hack Humphrey sat uncomfortably on the hospital stretcher. His behind was directly touching the paper sheet, and he could feel the air getting into the back of his gown. He looked at the closed door, and the fluorescent light hurt his eyes. Could this be any more undignified? He was a billionaire, for fuck's sake! He was used to people kissing his ass, not feel the breeze pass by it.

The door opened and Doctor Robert MacArthur entered. His lifelong friend looked worried, a deep crease furrowing his forehead. Hack's eyebrows pulled together as well, as if called by the other man's expression. *That's a wake face, but I'm not dead. Not yet, anyway.* His eyebrows pulled even closer.

Sensing his mood, Rob fixed his signature smile in place. "Are you still in those ridiculous clothes?" His mouth burst into the mocking laugh that always put Hack on edge.

"Nobody told me I could change, you ass. And what took you so long? I'm a busy man, in case you don't remember."

Hack jumped down from the stretcher and ripped the gown. His six-foot two-inch naked frame strode effortlessly to the bathroom and reappeared exactly twelve minutes later in a dark blue suit, a silver tie, and polished black leather shoes.

Rob whistled. "Who's getting married?"

"Not me. That's for sure. I have a meeting with the Brazilian ambassador. Tough negotiation, but we're getting there."

"Oh, Brazil: hot chicks and caipirinhas. I can imagine how hard that might be…"

Hack huffed. "C'mon. You already did the put-Hack-at-ease show. Now tell me what the hell is going on. I only came to see you for a cramp in my leg!"

Fake smile crumbling, the doc sat down on his chair with a plop, and Hack did the same on the other side of the maple-colored desk.

"Alright. Let me explain. When you came in for the cramp, I figured it could be a potassium deficiency, so I ordered the tests. But then, once you were here, I had to check the other basic numbers—it's standard procedure. While doing it, we found that you have a slight arrhythmia, your cholesterol levels are off the charts, and you have above average blood pressure."

"Meaning?"

"Meaning, you're a heart attack waiting to happen."

Hack sighed. "Oh man… I knew I shouldn't have come. So, can we fix this? Don't you have a pill I can take and get on with it?"

"Sure I do. Three of them, actually."

"You have the solution? Then why the wake face?"

Rob looked down, avoiding Hack's eyes, and took a pad. The handwriting was the one of a scribe, not an MD, and the pen was a gold and silver Mont Blanc. "Here are the prescriptions you need to take. One of each in the morning before breakfast. Come back in three months for another checkup." He slid the paper forward with his left hand while his right hand's fingertips tapped a rhythm on the table.

Hack's chin dipped for a second. Then he took the prescription, folded it and put it in the breast pocket of his shirt. Both men stood up and shook hands.

"Lunch at the club on Saturday?" Hack's bass voice sounded casual.

Rob grinned, his clown face back in place. "It depends. Are you paying?"

"Man, how can you be so cheap? Yes, I'm paying."

"Well, you pay off my debts and I buy lunch."

"No way. I buy lunch, you pay your debts."

"Alright, if you insist." A smirk pulled halfway up, and Rob's pupils shone with mischief.

"Twelve sharp. Don't make me wait or you pay."

"I'll be there." The doctor nodded, opening the door.

* * *

It was a sunny day, and the river sparkled cheerfully behind the golf course. Hack's fingers folded and unfolded the napkin distractedly, while his eyes roamed the low hills with greener than green grass.

His mind was somewhere else though.

Rob's message had been an odd one, and the whole situation would be highly entertaining if his health weren't on the line. His friend had tapped on the table in Morse code, soft so it wouldn't be heard. The cryptic message read:

"No take. T.I.P."

They hadn't used that kind of kiddy communication since they were children pretending to be spies. *Talk In Person.* What was he up to now?

At five after twelve, Rob appeared. The right corner of Hack's mouth twitched before his friend's choice of clothing. The polo shirt was a real *polo* shirt, a La Martina Russian Yellow Cab team shirt.

Sitting at the table, Rob pulled his cell phone, opened the back and took the battery out, sliding both pieces into the side pocket of his shorts. Hack lifted one eyebrow.

"Later. Let's eat."

The waiter appeared, bringing spicy bread, pâté and a bottle of Chamonard Morgon 2009, pouring a small amount into Hack's glass. Hack swirled the glass in front of his nose, took a small sip and nodded once. The maître served both glasses with graceful precision.

"What's on the menu today, Patrick?" Rob asked, after a brief glance at the name tag.

"Three courses, sir?"

Rob nodded emphatically.

"Just main course and dessert for me," Hack interrupted.

"In the seasonal cuisine, I can offer you a spicy bruschetta with flowers butter followed by quail with asparagus sauce, and a side of kuman sweet potatoes, purple carrots and nasturtium salad, right from our organic garden. In French cuisine, the creamy escargot soup is fantastic for an appetizer."

Hack controlled his need to pull a face when hearing *escargots*, but he was not going to be eating snails anytime soon. "Just sirloin with lion's mane mushrooms and a side of pomme noisette with cayenne pepper sauce for me, please. No salt."

"I'll take the seasonal menu, please," Rob added quickly, offering one of his toothpaste ad smiles.

When the waiter cleaned up the table and brought coffee, Rob changed his cheerful disposition. One minute he was giving very detailed explanations about different folkloric dance styles in South America, and the next, his mouth fell shut, and his eyes became glossy and haunted.

"Are you going to tell me what the hell is going on?"

"It's bad."

"Why? I'm not going to have a heart attack just now…"

"No. You don't understand. It's the side effects of the drugs I'm worried about. But I can't talk about it in the office. I am being watched, and I could lose my license."

"What?" Hack's face took a falcon quality.

Rob crouched forward, his eyes darting around.

"I don't know if I'm becoming paranoid, but I think they've been using my own phone to spy on me."

"If there's enough money on the table, they might. Now, are you going to tell me what's going on?"

A deep sigh left his friend's chest. "This is what happened. There's an agreement between the clinic and this new pharmaceutical company, Bymex LLC. If the tests come back positive for cholesterol, we have to prescribe their version of the statin drug. It seemed like a reasonable deal, and they lent the money for the new clinic downtown sans interest. It's a hundred-million-dollar project."

Hack's fingers raked his hair. "Clever. They have your bosses by the nuts."

Rob gave him a dirty look. "I've been prescribing it for a year, and it showed good results in older guys as protection from a second heart attack. But six months ago, the target group was extended. It has to be prescribed to both men and women of any age, with total cholesterol above the threshold, independent of previous cardiac issues. Right about then, one of my soccer buddies came to see me. Now, I could get into hellish trouble for saying what I'm about to say, so please do not repeat this to anyone…"

Hack nodded.

"I gave him the typical prescriptions to correct his numbers. They were similar to yours, but he had no arrhythmia. Two months later he came back because he had erectile problems. He was also gaining weight, and getting softer, losing his edge. We tested for testosterone and it was low. So I followed the clinic's recommended protocol and gave him a testosterone cream, also from the same company."

Rob took a deep breath, and Hack inhaled too. *This is it.*

"His balls and dick shrank." Rob let the air out.

Hack eyebrows shot up.

"I'm not kidding. This guy is forty-two and his life is over." Rob picked up his napkin from his lap and put it at the side of his plate with a theatrical movement.

"Have you spoken with your bosses about this?"

"Yes."

"And?"

Rob massaged his chin. "They recommended I read the literature and see how the possible rare side effects of these drugs are standard to all the brands. Roger went on to explain that we are heroes who do heroic medicine, and we are at war with sickness. And all wars damage the terrain and can provoke additional problems to be dealt with in the future."

"Is it true? Are they all the same?"

"I have no idea. All the papers sponsored by the industry I've read say the products are wonderful, and all the so-called *independent* studies say they are very dangerous, some even say they are also useless for the intended purpose."

"Interesting double whammy."

"Indeed." Rob sighed. "Someone is playing with the numbers, but I don't know enough to tell the difference."

"How independent are the independent studies?"

"I have no clue."

Lost in deep thought, Hack bobbed his head slowly from side to side. "What a brilliant business model. They create a hungry market, promote via authority, have the mediators in the pocket... I wish I could do something like that..."

Rob gawked at him, then smiled. "Interesting how you see the business side first, and the moral side later. On the other hand, your online store wins all the awards for quality and service. I think you do have a heart somewhere..."

A grin spread across Hack's face, and light sparkled in his deep blue eyes, HH LLC was one of the biggest online stores in the world, his pride and joy. "Let's keep it a secret and say it's just a business strategy." After glancing down for two heartbeats, he focused on his friend. "Alright. So I can't take those medicines, or my dick will fall off. Now, how do I solve the problem? Is it there a *non-heroic* path?"

"Only on the quack side." Slanting his lower lip, Rob took a paper and wrote a number. "I can't believe I'm doing this," he muttered, giving the paper to Hack. "This is the number of a guy who practices *functional medicine*." He quoted the air with his fingers when mentioning the last two words. "I lost one of my patients to him. This man was fifty, with the typical cholesterol/high blood pressure issue and his testosterone levels were going down fast. Recently I called him to see how he was doing. He said he had never felt better and his new wife was pregnant."

Chapter 2

Yani

A knock on the engraved door of the bank manager's office startled Yanina. It was followed by the fiery ochre of her mother's hair.

"Hello, darling. Ready for lunch?"

Plastering a fake smile, Yanina tried hard and failed to hide how annoying she found the intrusion. Her mother refused to acknowledge she was busy. A bank didn't run on its own, not even a small branch office like this one.

"I'm sorry, Mom. I can't. Didn't you see my message? There's work that can't be postponed."

Her mother smiled the same smile of hers, mirroring both her façade and her annoyance. María Adelia, Yani's mother, was an expert at the art of silent communication, and her daughter had been trained in this lady's sport since birth.

"This time I will have to insist, darling." The older woman punctuated each word while her eyes darted fire, and Yanina knew right away there was no escape.

"Alright," she agreed, standing up and picking up her purse.

After a short flight of steps and a couple of nods to specific people, they came out from the coolness of the bank and into the searing wet hot of the tropics. Cartagena de Indias was beautiful and hot, very hot, all year around.

The restaurant was just two blocks ahead, but they didn't walk. Being the family of a politician embroiled in a crusade against drugs in Colombia had its drawbacks, one of which was the need for bulletproof glass and bodyguards everywhere they went.

"So, what do we eat?" María Adelia looked at her daughter with mischief. "Shrimp ceviche?"

"Mom, I can't. I'm working."

"But you love it!"

"Yes, but I can't breathe close to anyone after eating it! I'm the manager for goodness sake! I can't stink of raw garlic!"

"You should take the day off then."

Yanina rolled her eyes. "Alright, ceviche it is. I can always use a mouthwash later, or maybe bleach…"

Giggling, the older woman called the waiter.

After the ceviche, they skipped the main course and had cholado for dessert, finishing with coffee. Yani loved to have cholado in this restaurant. It had caramel instead of condensed milk and ice cream instead of ice, the fruit salad was fantastic and the strawberry sauce to die for.

She sighed happily. It was good to be with her mother, and she loved food. It always brought memories of good times.

"Mom, I love having lunch with you, but I guess you didn't come all the way here just for the fun of it…"

The atmosphere morphed from cheerful to ominous while her mother took her phone out, selected a video and gave it silently to Yani.

The image showed a middle aged reporter talking gender violence against women, and how the last episodes were particularly brutal as they came from the government and their allies.

The image cut to a DEA official saying that Marcos Argüelles, the Comandante, had surrendered himself to the police and was facing one hundred and fifty years of prison.

The reporter asked the official if it was true that they had kidnapped his sister and raped her repeatedly, sending the recordings to Argüelles, until he surrendered. The man answered: "No comment."

It cut again toward the woman talking:

"It is a sad day for Colombia the day the government supports rape as a tool. Argüelles is not saint, there is no doubt about it, but he doesn't claim to be on the side of the righteous, as the government officials should be. Many rumors are circulating about the way the situation started, the strongest one mentioning Senator Miguel Suarez as the one who gave the location of Argüelles's sister to the anti-drug brigade. Let's all pray for his daughter Yanina, so she doesn't become the next victim of this dirty war."

Yani looked up from the phone right into her mother's eyes, her own transfixed into two pools of pain.

"Silvia?"

Her mother nodded and covered her mouth with her hand, lifting her face to the ceiling so the tears would not spill and ruin her makeup. Yani had seen her doing it uncountable times.

"Querida, you will have to leave. Your father has connections in our embassy in Uruguay. I know your job means the world to you, but…"

"Mom, it's Silvia we're talking about. Why did he do it? How could he?"

Her mother sighed. "You know why. His hate for Marcos supersedes common sense."

"I don't understand. It was ages ago, only one summer. We were teens. It started, it ended. What's the big deal?"

"He found out you gave the boy more than a kiss, darling. He doesn't forget or forgive those things."

Yanina blushed. "But…"

"Men like your father and Marcos are natural disasters. You can't ask a hurricane to be a breeze, nor waste time getting upset with it. You just cope and rebuild after the storm passes."

Yanina shook her head slowly, her fingers fidgeting with her bracelets.

"You will have to leave. Your father arranged accommodations for you in our embassy in Uruguay."

"How?"

"*Corcho*," her mother said, and her lower lip slid to a side showing her deep disgust for the situation.

Yanina knew right away there was more to the story.

"Mom… Besides being five feet tall, *Cork* is a power seeker cocaine addict and likes busty women in show-business. We have absolutely nothing in common."

"Yes, I know. And he knows we know. So he accepted to buy our silence with this favor."

"What exactly does this favor entail?"

"We are still negotiating, but you father is pushing for marriage."

"No way. Do you really want that life for me?"

"Sometimes, darling, we need to make hard decisions and live with the consequences. Marcos made a call to his people to get you and take you to one of his plantations. You know what happens to women in those places, don't you?"

She did, yet she didn't. No matter how hard she tried, she couldn't see in Marcos the monster everyone depicted. He wouldn't do that to her, would he?

"But can you picture it? Living with a man who doesn't love you? Who cheats on you? Who doesn't treat you right?"

"As a matter of fact, I do."

"What do you mean?"

María Adelia sighed.

"Let me tell you a little story," her mother said.

"The summer after you were born, I was still carrying some extra weight, my hands were swollen and the wedding ring was cutting in my finger. Your father helped me to take it off but was not happy about it. We were in a casino in Chile and Miguel was obsessed with playing roulette. I was bored, so I went to the bar for a drink, and a man approached me. I told him I was married, but he insisted on buying me a drink. I kept saying no, but he was drunk, so it became loud. Your father came and delivered his fist into the man's face."

Yanina covered her suddenly open mouth with both hands.

"He asked what he was thinking hitting on married women. The other man said he thought I was lying because I had no ring. That second his face morphed from righteous anger to white fury… against me. He took me forcefully by the arm and escorted me to our room. I thought he was going to hit me. But when we arrived, he calmly said that if I was going to disrespect him by not wearing his ring, from that moment forward he was not going to respect me either. He spent that night in another woman's arms, and it was only the first one of many. In retrospect, I think he just used it to punish me because I was still fat. You know how important neatness is for your father."

Yanina was gaping at her mother. "Why didn't you divorce him?"

"I tried. When we set foot on Colombian soil, I ran to my parents' house. My father, his soul rest in peace, sent me back."

"Grandpa? *Oh goodness.* How did you cope?"

"You were a baby. Providing for you was my main concern, and being with your father seemed to be the wisest option at the time. My education was a fine one but didn't include any useful skill. And later on… staying became my revenge. When you marry a man, you don't only marry him, but the life he offers. The life your father offers me is comfortable. I'm keeping it."

"But…"

"I honestly don't care about the other women. Maybe I should, but I just don't. When I need company, he is there. When I don't, he doesn't bother me. As long as I don't cheat on him and look nice, the arrangement works for both of us."

"Is that the life you want for me?"

"In retrospective, it hasn't been a bad life."

"And what about love?"

"What about it?"

* * *

With the heart pumping hard, Yani ran as if her life depended on it, and it did. Escaping through the tiny bathroom window was a teenager trick, but she was beyond caring about decorum at this stage. She was not marrying Cork, nor was she going to fall into Marcos's machinations.

It was hard to say what worried her the most; getting caught by the feared drug lord or her father. Her childhood memories with Marcos and Silvia in the summer house glossed over the dangerous man everyone else saw in him. But again, until she betrayed her father's expectations, he had been Prince Charming. And she preferred not to remember her last encounter with Marcos. It was too painful.

Entering a coffee shop, she headed to the restrooms, again, looking for a place to hide.

"I can't stay here forever…" she murmured.

Drawings of hearts slashed with arrows and manly body parts answered her silently from the stall door.

The noise coming from her phone was becoming unnerving, so she finally decided to check it. There were over ten messages. Some were from her parents, urging her to call them. Some from reporters, asking for an interview. And one from an unknown number she decided not to listen to.

The phone rang again, with a distinctive sound that always made her smile. On the screen her best friend's name, Marita, was winking at her.

"Hello."

"Yani? Are you alright?"

"Still in one piece, so I guess… yes."

"I was out in the boat all day, and when I came home, Enrique told me. I thought my heart would stop. What was your father thinking?"

Yani sighed. "I don't know…"

"What are you going to do?"

The sigh was even deeper. "I don't know…"

"Oh girly… ok, I know exactly what you are going to do."

"You do?" This piqued Yani's curiosity. Marita had a wild imagination, even wilder than her temperament and her hair, and that was saying something.

"Yes. We are leaving tomorrow in the sailboat. It's the trip to Cancun I told you about. You are coming with us as a stowaway and give everyone the slip."

"Do you have room in the boat for three?"

"Well... just a sec." Yani could hear muffled sounds. "I know this was supposed to be a romantic getaway... no, we are not having a threesome, you dick." The speaker was uncovered and Yani could hear the noise of breaking glass. Then the hand came back over the speaker. "She is my best friend and in danger... yes, alright, I will let you in there if you are on your best behavior with Yani. She is an innocent, get it?" The hand lifted from the speaker. "All set," Marita said.

Yani's face was a dark shade of red. "Uh oh, thanks but I'm not sure it's going to work."

"It will. Where are you? I'm picking you up right now, before something else happens."

Chapter 3

Hack

The waiting room was confusing. Soft music, cherrywood paneling, geode rocks cut in half guarding the most beautiful crystals, and spotlights over pointillist paintings of landscapes, gave the place the feeling of museum mixed up with spa. Even more confusing was the fact that it made Hack feel welcome. He was a high-tech kind of guy, and rocks had never been his thing, until now. He didn't have time to look around though. About a minute after his arrival, the office door opened, and a middle age man came out. Dr. Millman had a slight frame and wavy hair with some white on the sides. Hack noticed he didn't have the sunken eyes of most doctors, and his smile showed white but crooked front teeth—his own. He had a tan and moved with ease. One word came to mind: *Vitality.*

"Mr. Humphrey?"

"Yes."

"Is your wife joining us later?"

"I don't have one," Hack clipped irascibly. He didn't like the feeling of lack and inadequacy, and that simple question brought up both.

"Oh, I see. Come in, please." The doctor smiled, but Hack could sense tension in the answer. The man was not happy. *What the heck?*

It was funny—as in weird: one word from someone in a pseudo position of power showing something he didn't have, and he was a bulky eight-year-old again, unable to run fast enough and scolded by his father for it.

The office was decorated in a similar way of the waiting room, but the paintings were naïve, and there was a whiff of cigar. Completely different from what Hack considered professional, yet it worked.

Hack didn't want to feel at ease though. He didn't like this guy now that he had caught him lacking in something. He was one of the most eligible bachelors, and had been for the last fifteen years. He didn't have a wife because he didn't want to.

"Please sit down. Do you want anything to drink?"

"No, thank you."

"Alright. Let's cut to the chase. I have been looking into your tests…"

"Just one thing before we start."

"Yes?"

"I always require from my service providers full disclosure of earnings related with the business we have. I need to know what your earnings from the practice are, and what the extras that might involve me are. For example, the tests. Do you get any kick back? How about the medicines?"

The doctor smiled, amused. "I charge for the consultation, and I do sell some of the products I consider the best option for my clients. I also give conferences, organize cruise trips, own vacation cabins in strategic locations, and have a couple of books that made it onto the main local newspaper's bestseller list."

Impressive, but Hack didn't want to show it.

"And how much do you make yearly?"

"It's a six figures business."

Hack's fingertips tapped rhythmically the table. "You could triple the office side with just two adjustments. I called for a consultation and your secretary went back and forth three times with mine for the forms and two rounds of studies before seeing you."

"I know." The man smiled broadly.

"Why don't you do it within the consultations?"

"My clients are busy. I'm busy. More importantly: I'm in the business of health, not sickness management, my friend. Can we proceed now?"

"Yes, please."

Hack was genuinely impressed. A business that didn't do everything in its power to increase cash flow was unheard of. He thought he was the last ass who really put the customers and the crew first. He had refused to sell shares of his companies to keep full control over the procedures, especially when they hurt the bottom line. And now this guy…

It was awesome.

"About the form…" the doctor said, after studying some papers.

"Your secretary said it was not necessary to provide all the information if I didn't feel comfortable."

"But you didn't put anything in it…"

Hack brooded. The form was awfully indiscreet. He was not telling anyone about his personal life. Period.

"I don't feel comfortable sharing my personal life."

"I see. Did Robert tell you anything about the way functional medicine works?"

"No… he only said you'd helped a client with a problem similar to mine."

"Well, let me give you the Cliff Notes. In functional medicine, we start from the premise that the body is intelligent, wants to be healthy and does the best possible job for the conditions it's in.

"So to understand the root causes of a dysfunction we dive into the internal nutrition/poison elements on one hand, and the environmental conditions on the other."

Alright. So the guy was not just nosy. There was a reason behind the madness.

"I see. I did make a copy of the form and filled it in, but I prefer to keep it. It's been enlightening actually."

"I'm glad you did. I will tell you what I've learned of your life from the tests, and you can confirm or deny. The form and the tests are for the most part redundant for the right eye."

This piqued Hack's curiosity. It was like being with an investigator, or a *witch doctor.*

"Let me see… you are health conscious, eat organic and avoid fried foods for the most part, but you like your egg yolks and cheese. I would say a steak and potatoes kind of guy, but of the highest quality. You don't cook, eat out sometimes but have the food delivered mostly.

"You play golf socially, maybe for business. Always use sunscreen when playing. You also run regularly and swim. You have exclusive access to the pool and don't share it much.

"You are a workaholic, and work long hours, often after midnight. You work in a place with computers, WiFi or electric equipment in abundance. Your job is very stressful, but you are on top of it. You love it and find it exciting.

"How did I do?"

"Nicely done research." Hack smiled. "You know? Most of what you said can be gathered from a web search, but some details are really puzzling. How did you know I have my food delivered?"

"The hair analysis. It gives a fair account of the toxins you have been exposed to, and the mineral balance in your body."

"The wrapping paper and plastics leach toxins in the food?"

"You're fast. I like it."

"How about the golf?"

"You have some lawn pesticide residue and paint volatile residues, but not too much. Those are mostly used in California golf courses. You have aluminum toxicity and vitamin D deficiency, showing the use of extensive amounts of sunscreen. But your deficiency is not as bad as it should be; therefore, you eat free range chicken eggs with their yolks, and outdoorsy cattle produce."

"And the pool?"

"There are residues of chlorine, but not of some byproducts that appear when it reacts chemically with human urine. So my take is… it's a private pool. I don't know what part of the human mind acts there, but it's impossible to keep people from peeing."

Hack was starting to find the guy fascinating. Bizarre, but fascinating.

"So… what's wrong with me?"

"The usual… you are poisoned, have diverse nutritional deficiencies, have bought into the low sodium myth, live in a soup of electromagnetic fields and your circadian rhythms are not being treated with the respect they require."

"You mean, salt is good?"

"Table salt is to real sea salt like white sugar to sugar cane. Table salt is really bad for you; sea salt is a rich nutrient."

"And how about the heart attack?"

"What heart attack?"

"Didn't you see my numbers? High blood pressure, high cholesterol, and arrhythmia…"

"The arrhythmia could be due to many things, but my bet is on mineral deficiency. The high cholesterol… could be just part of the inflammatory process or mouth infections. Usually all those numbers go towards the individual optimal values when balance is attained. In your case, I do expect a higher general cholesterol than the norm, as it happens with high IQ people."

"So… no risk of heart attack?"

"Well, I would need to order some more tests to make sure of that. Usually a heart attack shows necrosis of small areas of the heart as precursor. But I prefer to address the general situation first, then we can go to the specifics if needed. Once the body is clean and nourished, it usually takes care of everything else."

"So what do I do?"

"Good question. I can summarize it in one phrase: get a wife."

"What?" The dear in the lights look in Hack's face was priceless. The doctor couldn't restrain a chuckle.

"My good man… you need real food, the kind that takes several hours to cook. You need someone you want to go to bed early with and take vacations with, you need someone that blesses your heart and kicks your behind in that sweet way only old-fashioned ladies can."

Hack shook his head and lifted the right corner of his mouth. Rob's mom was exactly like that.

"Do you have one for sale?" Now the smile turned into a smirk.

The doctor laughed. "No, my friend. Not everything has a price tag. Shocking, I know…"

"Well, I don't have a wife, and the lady you mention is almost an extinct species, so can you help me with my condition or not?"

The man sighed.

"Let's see what you are willing to change, and work around those things that you can't. Alright?"

"Sounds like a plan."

"It all starts with a vacation…"

Chapter 4

Yani

"If Paradise were a place, it would be just like this," Yani murmured into the soft breeze, as her body floated with ease in the translucent waters.

Marita and Francisco were back at the boat, enjoying their vacation as planned—which essentially meant sex and more sex. So she stayed on the beach most of the time to give them some privacy. The cove was a beautiful place of transparent emerald sea kissing softly impalpable white sand and crowned by jungle and mountains. It couldn't be accessed by land, and it was away from most tourist circuits.

She felt safe here. She felt at peace.

"If only I could stay here forever…" her eyes settled on the empty cabin. From a distance it looked small and round, almost like an igloo made out of clay and, oddly enough, wine bottles. Surrounded by banana trees, it had a water collecting system and solar panels. The perfect hideout for a modern hermit.

The noise started very low and became louder and louder. Yani looked around and saw it: a small dot in the sky. A helicopter was coming. Her eyes zeroed on the jet ski, but if they were coming for her, the last thing she wanted was to put her friends in harm's way.

The jungle was not an option.

The water was not an option.

Her perfect refuge had transformed in a heartbeat in a mousetrap.

Yani ran toward the cabin and sat on the floor of the curvy entryway, her back glued the low wall, her legs against her chest. The sun was coming through the glass bricks and painted the terracotta floor with polka dots in green and blue.

She could hear the helicopter landing close, and panic rose up her throat. It couldn't be. How did he find her? She closed her eyes tight and froze.

"Miss, please stand up. This is private property. You're trespassing," Trespassing? Yani heard the almost-disguised Texas drawl and her heart flip-flopped. Gringos? Not her father or Marcos' goons? Trespassing? Her head turned toward the voice and found the barrel of a rifle pointing to the ground, then two hands expertly holding it in front of a pair of cargo pants. Looking higher, she found a corded torso shaped with real work, not in the gym, and going even higher, she saw a square face and alert brown eyes totally focused on her.

Very slowly and deliberately, she stood to find herself still dwarfed by the man. He was two heads taller than her. Her hands ironed the folds of her bikini skirt.

"What's going on?" Yani heard another man inquiring.

"Please stay behind, sir. There's a woman."

The other man entered anyway and Yani found herself looking into the most hypnotic ice-blue eyes she'd ever seen.

"Cómo te llamas?" he asked for her name in that funny Donald Duck accent so common with gringos.

"Neighbor," she answered in English.

"Huh?"

"I'm your neighbor. From the boat? Sorry for trespassing. The noise scared me."

She managed an apologetic smile and extended her right hand for a handshake.

The man took it, but didn't shake, just held it. She felt heat and the hint of an electric current climbing up her arm, into her shoulder, and from there it snaked fast toward her belly. *What the heck?*

"Pleased to meet you." His eyes bored into hers and, for a second, she felt she could melt.

"Well, I'd better be going…" She tried to disentangle, but he didn't let go of her hand.

"Neighbor, hm? Why don't you show me around while my guys set up camp?"

"Mmm sure…"

They walked on the beach toward the ocean, until the surf licked their feet.

"So?" he asked, smiling boyishly.

"What?"

"Show me around…"

"Oh…" She chuckled. He was fun for an older scary guy with goons, who was also two heads above her eye level—*what do these guys eat to be so tall?* She actually knew exactly what they ate up north, having lived in the US for a couple of years. That food didn't help her grow in height, only sideways.

"In front you have the warm turquoise waters of the Caribbean, and over there my boat," she announced in her best imitation of a tourist guide. "The cove can only be accessed by water or air, as you already know." She turned to see the cabin and the four guys moving things around. "Over here your cabin, and your men doing…whatever they are doing. Behind them, the jungle and mountains, which soon will be framing one of many perfect sunsets."

"Thank you." He nodded.

"You are very welcome." She added a tiny curtsy to her nod.

"What's your name?"

"I don't want to tell you my name, nor want to know yours."

"You don't know who I am?"

"Nope."

To his surprised smiled, she added: "Shocking, I know."

"Hm?"

"The goons…"

"Oh, right."

Do you know who I am?"

"Nope."

"Perfect."

They both grinned. This was going to be fun.

* * *

Yani felt rather than saw the man arrive at the shore.

"You woke up early," he commented, sitting by her side.

"You too," she shot back.

"Yeah, I have to start the day with sun gazing. What's your excuse?"

"What's sun gazing?"

"Just watch the sunrise, until ten degrees more or less."

"Oh…"

"So?"

"So what?"

"What are you doing up so early?"

"I share the boat with two friends who are a couple. I try to give them as much space as possible."

His mouth rounded, and his eyes sparkled. He also changed position, lifting his knees.

Yani didn't dare to look, but it was obvious her comment had caused a physical reaction.

"So you're at the beach all day?"

"As much as possible. I hope you don't mind."

He grinned, and she felt her pulse rushing. "Not at all."

She had to say something. Make it clear she was not for the taking before things got out of control…

"Look… the sun," he interrupted.

The man stood up, offering his hand to her. "Let's try this," he said.

He straightened his spine and started breathing slowly and rhythmically. Yani followed suit. She loved watching the sunrise, but this was a completely different experience. She could sense the light surrounding her and coming into her being when she inhaled. She could feel his hand around hers and his heat, hers, the sun, the breeze, the water and the land all joined in perfect harmony.

"I think that's enough," he said, still holding her hand. The whole process took about ten minutes.

"I'm honestly surprised," Yani told the man with no name. Her chest felt warm, his hand felt right around hers. The moment was intimate, and powerful, and completely unexpected.

He let go of her hand and scratched the back of his neck, as if ashamed of what had happened.

"I'm going for a run now."

"Ok. Have fun."

He smiled awkwardly and took off. Yani sat back on the sand. *What just happened?*

Chapter 5

Hack

Hack ran along the shore trying to collect his thoughts. *What just happened?*

He'd had the most intimate moment of his life with a woman he didn't know. *I don't even know her name, for fuck's sake!*

He wondered if this unusual experience was triggered by the sun and the beach or she had a role. In other words: would it have been the same way alone, with any woman, or this girl was special?

He could feel the energy coursing through his body, giving him a stamina he hadn't had an hour before. He was not a religious or very spiritual guy. Almost as a survival technique, he had chosen to keep his attention within the realm of what he could see and touch. But this… had been completely different. It felt so right. *She* felt so right. *So this is how life is supposed to feel…*

* * *

Yani

"Enjoying the view?" Smirking, Marita sat beside Yani with her legs hanging from the deck of the sailboat. Yani was watching their new neighbor.

"He is the most beautiful man I've ever seen…"

"You need to go out more."

Yani giggled. "You are right about that."

"What's his name?"

"I have no idea. Hot Hunk?"

Both girls laughed.

"HH for short? Definitely suits him." Marita's head slanted, her freckled nose wrinkled. "He is a bit old for you."

"Maybe. He's a great view anyway…"

"Go for it!" Marita winked.

"Of course not!" Yani answered, blushing.

"Why not?"

They heard noises and Marita gave her friend an apologetic smile before scurrying inside the cabin.

Why not? Because I don't do that stuff, and he chickened out on me. That's why. Still a great view. Yani sighed and resumed her observation.

* * *

Hack

Coming back, he didn't find the girl at the beach.

He'd seen her on the boat at noon. But when he came out from his scheduled nap, she was nowhere to be found.

Hack looked for Renton, his chief of security. The man was barbecuing a lizard. The leathery blueish meat didn't smell bad at all. Two of his men sat by the small fire, the third one was on guard, somewhere around.

"News?"

"Not much to hunt. Just birds and snakes. Lots of fruit and edible plants. It looks wild, but this is a carefully planned food and medicine forest. If delivery cuts out, we can make it. I climbed the hill to get a better view. We could go back on foot if necessary, but definitely not an easy route. The neighbor's story seems genuine so far. She now moved to the southern area and tried to stay out of sight. The other two remained at the boat all day…"

"Fucking like rabbits?"

"That would be an accurate description, sir."

"Do we have a habitational issue? Not much room inside the hut," Hack changed the subject.

"No problem. There is a back room in case of emergency. But we've already set up camp."

Renton looked up and Hack followed. There were hammocks and a camouflaged structure up in the trees.

"Impressive."

"The bones were already in place. Also, most coconut trees have steps, and there's a system of ropes interconnecting them. Very well built and disguised."

One of the guys grinned and went around the hut. He came back two minutes later with four chilled green coconuts. With three expert cuts of his machete, he opened a hole and passed the coconut to Hack.

He drank and the *feeling* more than the taste surprised him. There was a living quality to it.

"This is good..."

The men nodded.

"Is she still there?"

Renton nodded again, passing him his open but untouched coconut. Hack nodded back.

Hack walked all the way to the corner where the girl was hiding and sat by her side.

Her eyes drifted sideways and zeroed on the ocean again, ignoring him.

He put the coconut in front of her as a peace offering.

"Forgive me?" he tried. Rob's dad always used to say regarding women: *when in doubt, always apologize.*

"For what?" she asked, with a hint of surprise, but smiling.

Hack pushed his chin forward and let it set back in place. "I don't know. You tell me."

Her back straightened into somewhat of a fighting stance.

"There's nothing to forgive. After you ran away this morning, I thought it was better to give you some space."

"Oh," Hack gave a swing to his coconut. "so you are upset because I went for a run? It was on my schedule."

Her head snapped toward him and her eyes closed half-mast. "Please don't waste my time."

Hack sighed. "Alright. The feeling I got from sun-gazing was unexpectedly strong. It took me off guard, and I chickened out."

She nodded. "And this is why I decided to give you space."

"It wasn't because it scared the crap out of you too, was it? Who's wasting who's time now?"

"Look!"

"Just drink. Please?"

She took the coconut with both hands and drank. A line of juice fell down her chin, along her neck and into her cleavage. Hack was a split second from diving in and licking it all off. *Man, you're screwed.*

The girl placed the coconut on the sand, took a paper towel from her cooler and cleaned herself up.

"It's very good. Thank you."

"You're welcome."

There was an awkward moment of silence.

"Well, I should go. It's late."

She stood and he followed, picking up her cooler.

"So, tomorrow before dawn?" he asked, pushing her jet ski into the water until it floated.

"You want to do it again?" Surprise rounded her beautiful green eyes.

"Of course!" He grinned.

"Ok…" She smiled timidly back.

Chapter 6

Hack

It was sunrise and she was not there. A pang of anguish threatened to appear. He pushed it down and anger took its place. *Ridiculous.* Hack's analytical mind jumped at the opportunity, cheering him up. *Perfect. Now I'll know if what I felt yesterday was only the environment or if the girl was involved.*

The sun popped from behind the water and he started his breathing exercises. It was good. It was powerful. It was not the same.

Coming back from his run, he saw Mackey, one of his men, on top of a set of boulders. Underneath, the water had created a cave. The man gave him the thumbs up.

"Nice climb. Did you need gear?"

The guard let a rope down and slid with ease. They touched fists as salutation and the man gave Hack a laminated set of cards that read *Activities.*

"There are hooks on the rock. Three proposed routes of different difficulty. This is a cool place, sir."

"Glad you approve. We all needed a vacation, isn't it?"

Mackey grinned.

Hack looked at the cards and followed the instructions, finding the easy way up. It was a path hidden in the rocks, but it actually could be climbed with no gear by almost anyone.

"Girl's coming to shore," his man mentioned after scanning the ocean with his binoculars.

"Can you bring brunch up here? For two?"

"Sure." Mackey nodded, fruitlessly trying to hide a smile.

* * *

Yani

Yani arrived at the shore, feeling guilty. She'd said she would meet him at sunrise and couldn't make it. He sat by a palm tree in her new personal spot, reading a book.

"Hey, sorry I'm late." She tried her best nonchalant face.

"No problem," he answered with a smile that didn't reach his eyes.

She blew a raspberry. "I know you're upset. I can feel it."

She was angry now.

He cocked his head and arched one brow. "I'm sorry?"

She giggled. "Want to know what happened?"

"I'm curious. Yes."

"We stayed late with my friends and had some drinks, so I overslept."

He looked at her sharply. "You shouldn't drive the jet ski wasted. It's very dangerous."

Now it was her time to cock her head and lift an eyebrow. "Do I look wasted?"

He stood up and approached her. His hand took her jaw and he examined her eyes.

"Does your head hurt?"

"I said I'm not wasted. Can I have my face back, please?"

"Sorry…" he said, releasing her.

"What are you reading?" she asked, chirpy. *What in the world are you doing? Flirting?.*

"Tragedy and hope," he said, taking a bookmark from the front cover and placing it on the page he was reading. It was made of glossy deep blue cardboard and read HH LLC. Yani couldn't hide the smile. Of course she knew HHLLC was one of the biggest online stores in the world. She bought most of her books there too. She never knew what the letters meant, though. In her mind, it became *Hot Hunk* LLC. Too funny.

"Oh." She bobbed her head a couple of times. The name of the book didn't register.

"It's a history book."

"Oh nice." Now her smile was genuine, and curiosity sparked from her eyes.

"Do you like to read?" he asked.

"Yeah, but I'm more of a tablet app kind of girl lately. I do love paper, but it's a lot easier to buy this way."

"Yeah, I get you. I'm in a low-tech vacation. Therefore the paper book."

"Oh…"

Stillness extended between them. Yani could almost hear the ticking of a clock. It reminded her of the wind-up grandfather clock back at her parents' house. It was a huge noisy beast from the late eighteen hundreds.

"Hey, do you have any plans for today?" his voice broke the silence.

"Not really. Why?" Relief washed over her.

"Have brunch with me?" His smile was contagious.

"Sure."

"Ok, let's go," he said, taking her hand.

They walked along the beach to the rocks. Yani had seen them from afar, but never dared to come this way before. They were humongous boulders, some taller than a house, setup in a tight maze. Lichen carpeted the sides in the shadier areas, and she could hear bird chatter.

He led her around the boulders to the other side. The water was at her knees and she noticed a mild current. It felt dangerous.

He saw her hesitation. "Trust me?"

"Have you been here before?"

"Yes."

"Then yes."

He grinned again, took her hand and kept walking. Yani felt something soft and warm spreading from the center of her chest. Something she couldn't put a name on and didn't exactly belong to her. It was mostly his, but she was happy to be there for the ride. In moments like this, being empathic paid off big time.

"Ok, here we are. This is the easy route up. You go first."

Her scared look must have been amusing, considering his condescending smile.

"Look. There are handholds in the rock, and see the red dots? They show the way."

"Oh." Yani could see it now. The whole path was marked. It actually looked doable. And fun.

She started climbing, cautious of where she put hands and feet. Halfway up, she realized it was actually easy, but she also felt tired.

"Use your legs' strength. Hands only for support."

"Alright," she answered and twisted her head to look at him.

His face was just an inch from her butt. Talking about giving him a view. Her cheeks felt hot. She was probably red to her ears. His eyes flashed with devilment.

"Almost there," he said, and she could feel his breath in the back of her thighs.

The rest of the climb went in a blur. Embarrassment pushed her up at fast speed, especially when his chest bumped in her rear.

The top of the boulder was a terrace. Standing, she could see the cove, the cape in the distance, the boat, the jungle. Everything.

"Wow." Yani felt she'd set foot on the top of the world. She was breathing hard. Her arms and legs hurt. And it was so worth it.

He stepped behind her back, very close but without touching her. She could feel the heat of his broad chest soaking into her skin. She wanted him to hug her, to kiss her neck, to...

His hands encased her waist and she bit her lip. She felt like a teenager again. Fresh and careless and happy.

"Hungry?" he asked huskily in her ear.

She turned to see again that impish smile of his.

Her mouth twitched to one side, and he chuckled.

He turned, making her turn with him, and she saw a cooler in the middle of the boulder.

"You really brought food? Up here?"

"Let's see…"

They walked hand in hand to the cooler and he retrieved two green coconuts, two banana leaves folded into boats with a salad of fish, veggies and red rice soaked in coconut milk sauce, and two wood forks.

They sat on a protruding rock that looked completely natural, but Yani doubted it had appeared there on its own. He was right by her side, his leg touching hers.

"This place is weird," she mentioned.

"Indeed. Nature has been touched here and there to make the space safe and comfortable, but without overwhelming her."

"Makes you wonder why we don't live like this…"

"Oh I know why… At this moment I'm just happy to be here, with you."

She smiled when his finger caressed her jaw. The warm fuzzy feeling was there again.

A second later the touch was gone, and he was attacking his food with vengeance. It was her cue to eat too. Climbing did work up an appetite.

Chapter 7

Hack

By the shore, the girl was already taking in the first rays of the living light. With her hair and cover-up tunic flowing in the wind, she was a vision. He placed himself on her back and hugged her. She laid her head on his shoulder and kept breathing.

Hack fell into the flow easily. With his chest to her back, they synchronized naturally. The energy flooded his system, and this time he was ready for it. The feeling of intimacy was deeper than the previous time, and he was also ready for it.

"It's enough," he murmured into her ear when the sun was five fingers above the line of the horizon.

"Hmm?" Her head turned towards the sound, and he placed his hand softly on her nape. She seemed in a light trance, and he didn't want to break it. He felt quite out of it himself.

His mouth closed the distance slowly, giving her time to retreat, until their noses touched. She didn't move, and his lips touched hers with a soft caress.

Now, she reacted. Her head recoiled and she placed her forehead on his shoulder, ruling out any chance of deepening the kiss, but not pushing him away either. He held her without words, giving her time to regain her balance. He'd never had a woman who's programming was triggered so early. And most were just faking it. Was she a virgin? *God, I hope not.*

* * *

Yani

"I have to go," she whispered.

Hack put his index finger under her chin and encouraged her to look into his eyes.

"Are you running away?" he joked.

"Er… yes," she acknowledged.

He released her from the hug but took her hand. "Let's go for a walk. I have a surprise."

"Sorry, but I can't."

"It's just a kiss."

"It's a statement of intent."

"Wow that sounds important. What's the application for?"

She giggled. "Stop laughing at me!"

"Let's go for a walk."

She shook her head.

"Please?"

She sighed. "Alright…"

For a second, Yani felt upset with herself for being such a meek little lamb. She wasn't into flings, but she really liked the guy. And she couldn't go back to the boat. So, what options did she have? Push him away and spend the rest of his vacation brooding at each other from afar, or trying to find some common ground…

They walked all the way to the boulders again, but this time they followed a wandering path at ground level that took them into the cave. Yani couldn't believe her eyes. It was breathtaking. A waterfall poured into a natural lake covered with white sand. Toward the front of the cave, there was a pool in the rock formed by the entering ocean water. Tiny fish of different colors moved between anemones, which resembled a bouquet of exotic flowers.

Yani looked at the man, confused. The scenery had a dreamlike quality, yet something was askew.

"Where is the light coming from?"

He arched one brow and smiled. "Light fixtures. Watch carefully."

She looked at the walls and the combed ceiling and saw recessed lamps with five petal flowers protruding from the entangled rocks.

"Solar panels?"

"Nope. Look again."

Then it hit her. They were… "Soda bottles?"

"Indeed. Half is exposed to the sun, half comes down here and they are filled with water and bleach. The light changes during the day as the sun hits different spots. Ingenious, isn't it?"

"I'm speechless. How did you know?"

"It's in the flyer. Swim with me?"

He didn't wait for her to answer. He just took his shirt off and jumped in.

She followed without thinking. The water was cool and the sand, powdery thin. The walls displayed a dancing pattern of lights and shadows.

He dove toward her, picked her up and draped her over his shoulder, striding to the waterfall. Yani was laughing, pummeling his back and screaming all at the same time.

He let her slide down his front until their heads were at the same level. The waterfall felt like a warm rain falling on her back. This time, it was Yani who kissed him. With her arms around his nape, her closed lips kneaded his. His tongue came out tentatively, and she sucked it in. Her legs wrapped around his waist and he grunted, his fingers closing on her butt.

She felt all of him, and she was ready.

She was so ready…

"Wait!" she exclaimed, cutting off the kiss.

"What?" He was breathing hard, just as she was.

"I can't do this…"

He sighed heavily. "Alright…"

He walked with her in his arms, her legs around his waist, and his hands on her butt toward the shallower part of the pool.

When the water was at his knees, he let her go and they sat on the rocks with their feet still in the water.

"I'm sorry if I led you on."

"You didn't. I just took my chances."

"Oh. Back there… I…"

"You almost overcame your programming. *Almost* being the keyword."

"I'm not that kind of girl," she murmured, her head down.

"The kind that owns her body and does what she really wants with it?"

Anger spread from her chest up her neck and face. She was probably red again. No woman likes to be called a zombie for not wanting to have sex, even if she did want to have sex. *It's complicated.* Some women could afford to give in to the moment and not think about the next day. She couldn't. She sat straight as if ready for war. But true to her upbringing, she took the high road.

"That was mean spirited."

He seemed surprised by her comment, his own aggressive pose dissipating completely.

"I know. Sorry. It's just frustration talking."

He stretched. "It's humbling though. I usually have to fend women off, and the ones I do take in are very accommodating."

"Let me see… you chase away fortune groupies and sleep with prostitutes?"

"Pretty much. Yes."

"Sorry I don't enter either of the categories."

Her smirk made him chuckle.

"You are not sorry. And, despite the sexual frustration, I'm actually happy about it too."

She smiled genuinely now.

"Are you one of those who needs commitment? Or what are the limits you set for yourself?" he asked simply, as if this were just business.

She thought about it for a minute before answering.

"I haven't actually decided it. I do know I'm not into flings."

"Why not?"

"Women can't separate the heart and the body. Well, at least I can't. Back there it was not only sensual. My heart was engaging too."

"Oh…"

"And as I see it, if I let it happen and we actually have sex… well, the outcome can only lead to heartache."

"Gotcha. If you don't like it you feel used, and if you like it you suffer because of the expiration date."

"Exactly. It took me five years to get over my first boyfriend. I can't afford to waste another five years. I'm thirty now. My biological clock is ticking."

"So you want to marry? Have kids?" There was a hint of interest in his eyes.

"So far, I haven't thought about it, but… I think I do. I love children."

He sank deep into introspection for fifteen long seconds.

"Do you like to cook?"

"I love it! Why?"

The man chuckled.

"What?"

"Nothing. Let's go back."

He held his hand and she took it.

"Thanks."

"You are very welcome."

Chapter 8

Hack

The knock at the door was loud and short, just two hits. Hack opened right away, as he was already on his way out, finding Renton on the other side.

"News?" Hack asked dryly.

"A tropical storm is heading our way. We are only at the tail, but outdoor activities will have to be restricted," the man answered succinctly.

"Understood. How prepared are we for it?"

"Well enough. Construction's sturdy. There are aluminum shutters for doors, windows and solar panels. The utility room can work as temporary shelter for the team. We have food for four days, a generator and replacement solar panels in case they break."

"Communications?"

"Working."

"When is it arriving?"

"This evening."

"Recommendations?"

"We can weather it with no issues and tomorrow will be over. The boat will not be safe as cover."

"Do we have room for three more?"

"Not at the back."

"Understood. Thank you."

The man nodded and left.

So it was up to him to invite the neighbors in. *Hmm.*

* * *

Yani

Marita interrupted Yani's wandering thoughts. She emerged from the cabin with Enrique in tow, carrying a waterproof handbag.

"We are going to town to grab a bite and spend the day. Are you coming?"

"Nah... I'll stay here. You two have fun."

Marita seemed worried. "Are you sure?"

"Yes, go. Spend the night over there too. I'll be fine."

"But..."

"Just go. You need your vacation, and I need time alone..."

Enrique put a phone in Yani's hand. "Speed dial one and we are here in less than one hour, got it?"

Yani looked up into Enrique's enthralling brown eyes. "Thanks, for everything."

He smiled and jumped onto the rubber boat, turning the motor on. Marita climbed in behind him, and soon they were just a dot in the distance.

Yani decided to stay in the boat. Yesterday she had been a split second from jumping the guy's bones, and she didn't even know his name. That had never ever happened to her, and she was not sure if she would be able to resist him the next time. Maybe it had to happen. *No.*

* * *

Hack

Hack waited for the girl to no avail. *She's not coming.*

He didn't feel like sungazing this morning. The omen of the storm and the fact the little lady was not there had clouded his mood. He was afraid he'd pushed her too far. But actually, he was pushing himself, not her. He'd never romanced a woman. He'd never had to, so his pride was at stake. She was so perfect for him, and it'd been over two weeks sans sex, and… *She likes to cook.*

It would be nice to take it slow. Let need develop at its own pace. She was right about flings and expiration dates. It was messy. Problem was, even when she kept denying her body to him, their hearts were already starting to engage, as she put it. So they were both in deep shit anyway.

True to his Spartan upbringing, he did his duty nonetheless and then went for a run. He climbed the boulders using the most difficult route to tire his body and empty his mind.

It wasn't working. He felt restless.

The breeze picked up and Hack looked at the ocean behind the cape, where a huge cloud grew from the water like a ten-story office building to widen on top into a convoluted field of lights and blue-hued shadows.

"That can't be good."

Renton came his way.

"Storm is coming faster?"

"Yes."

"The neighbors?"

"Just the girl. The other two left early."

"Where is she?"

"Diving."

Oh Jesus.

"Put air in the rubber boat and have it ready. I'll go ahead and swim to the boat."

"Ocean's starting to shake."

"Then we'd better hurry up."

Chapter 9

Yani

Seated on the floury sand, Yani played with the grey angelfish that had fearlessly approached her hand. Behind some rocks, a sea turtle observed her with sleepy, ancient wisdom. The reef was a bit further, but she didn't go. Swimming alone was a really bad idea, so she decided to keep the boat in sight the whole time.

She needed the peace that reigned under the surface to think. His questions the day before had been genuine and didn't have an answer. She hadn't had many chances to actually decide how far she would go with a man or how to pace it. It had been Marcos and this, with a long intermediate period of heartache, working her life away like an addiction, and guys asking her out and not showing up to the first date.

One thing was clear: she wanted this man. She wanted him more than she'd ever wanted her teenage sweetheart.

With Marcos, it had been more a story of him pushing for intimacy and her surrendering so he wouldn't be mad at her. But she'd never had a real visceral need for him, like she had now.

This was completely different.

He was romancing both her mind and her body *at the same time*. She really liked being with him, his sense of humor, his wit, how fast he understood situations, how he could control himself and, of course, he was a treat to look at. But it was also primal. When he touched her, she wanted it all. She'd even fantasized about him taking her by force so she could have him and keep her denial. And of course she knew he would never do it. If he were willing to do it, she would hate him. *Hypocrite.* Right there she understood that if he was still willing, she would do it. She deserved better than hoping to be a victim. Yanina decided to honor her body, and if her body wanted this man as much as her heart already did... so be it.

When Yani surfaced from her snorkeling session and climbed the boat to take her favorite place facing the shore, she saw the neighbor swimming toward her. *He is coming for me?*

Forearms on the rail of the boat, she looked at him, mesmerized. There was a rhythm, an almost hypnotic lullaby, in the way he propelled his powerful body through the waters. This, more than anything else, told Yani that something was wrong. He suddenly stopped in mid stroke and went under. He emerged again, but the movements were desperate, erratic. *He's drowning!* Yani didn't even think. She grabbed the life jacket and jumped onto the jet ski. In under a minute, she was with the man that haunted her thoughts, who now was contorting in pain.

"What happened?" she asked when he grabbed the jet ski for support.

"A cramp," he spat between tight teeth.

"Don't worry, I've got you," Yani said, with more heart than method, jumping into the water with him and securing the life jacket. How do you make over two hundred pounds of shaking muscle climb onto the jet ski? Well, at least he was not going to drown.

His big paw clamped on her arm and she panicked, kicking the jet ski, which started to float away. He moved fast, grabbing the seat with one hand and bringing her to his chest. She didn't have a life jacket, and they were far from shore and the boat.

"Thank you." His eyes were warm, warm and sincere. He also seemed relieved.

"Don't thank me yet. We still need to take you to shore in one piece... how's the cramp?"

"Manageable. C'mon," he said, and Yani flew in the air and found herself on the jet ski again. He climbed up behind her.

Still spooked by the whole situation, she turned on the engine with shaky hands.

He was right behind her, hugging her waist.

"Let's take you to shore."

"A storm is coming."

She looked at the wall of clouds for the first time and swallowed hard.

"O my gosh. I need to call Marita."

"I'll go with you."

When they arrived at the boat, Enrique's phone had five missed calls and ten messages. All related to an incoming storm. She called him.

"Por fin! Is the neighbor there?"

"Yes."

"Put the speaker on, please. I need to talk to him."

Yani was surprised but followed the instructions.

"Speaking," HH said.

"Hey, man. You heard about the storm?"

"Yes."

"We're stuck here. Have you ever sailed? Can you help us out?"

"Yes. What do you need?"

"The boat has a second anchor. It needs to be down. There is a rubber cover, and wood planks to fix it in place. Ask Yani for it and the screwdriver."

"Alright."

"One more thing…"

"Yes?"

"You'll have to take my sister in. You hurt her and I'll personally break your neck, no matter how many goons you have or how big you are. Get it?"

"Understood. Anything else?"

Yani's jaw went slack. What had Enrique just said?

"No. We'll be there tomorrow as soon as it clears up."

"Alright. Bye."

"Bye," Enrique answered, and cut the phone.

Yani was still gaping. The man just grinned and winked.

He turned and made some hand signals toward his cabin. Right away, two men pulled a rubber boat toward the ocean.

"So your name is Janice…"

Janice? Of course, that's how Yani might have sounded in his ears.

"What's yours?" she countered, neither accepting nor denying.

He seemed to think for a second too long. "William."

Yani didn't buy it but didn't feel like arguing after her own half-lie. *Ok, William, you'll stay Hot Hunk in my mind. HH for short.*

"Let's get this done. There's not much time," he added after having another look at the clouds. The serene waters of the cove were starting to shake, and the sky frowned menacingly at them. While HH climbed toward the flying bridge, Yani went into the cabin.

She picked up some clothes, hygiene basics and towels. Put them into two bags and took them to the cockpit. She also bagged the glass bottles to throw them overboard and locked everything else to reduce mayhem.

"Found the cover?" He asked while the engines roared and the boat started to move.

"What are you doing?"

"This area will get hit with too much debris. Further south will give it a better chance."

She climbed down into the cabin again, opened the side closets and located the rubber cover, screwdriver, screws, bolts and boards.

The wind was seriously picking up now, and the sea was shaking the boat. She could hear thunderstorms in the distance, and panic was starting to crawl along her spine.

The noise of steps was followed by legs, which were followed by two tall men slouching under the low ceiling of the cabin.

She signaled the closets, and they didn't need any more directions.

"Please go outside, ma'am."

She nodded and ran outside, where the winds could be heard howling in the distance and thick drops of rain were starting to fall.

"It's coming. Let's go." He picked her up unceremoniously and jumped into the rubber boat. Her stuff was already there, and she could see the men covering the flybridge and moving their way toward deck and cockpit at the same time.

"Your men?" she asked when he turned on the engine.

"They'll take the jet ski. You're probably going to lose it."

"I know," she murmured, her eyes locked on the humongous wall of clouds heading their way.

The boat crossed the angry waters at dazzling pace, and Yani had to lie flat under the benches to prevent herself from being launched.

As soon as they touched the sand, two men attached the launching wheels and hauled the boat at full speed toward the cabin, while she and HH ran by their side. He had picked up her bags and they had locked arms to anchor her at the same time. The wind was strong enough to make her loose her footing. The thought of being lifted by the swirling air and smashed someplace else caused panic to flood her system. They were running for their lives, literally.

Chapter 10

Hack

"What do you have here? A dead body?" Hack asked through gritted teeth when they finally got into the cabin.

"Oh goodness! You brought that? I threw it overboard!"

"I thought it had fallen."

"I'm sorry."

"So it *is* a dead body…" Hack insisted, even when the rattling noise of the bag had told him otherwise.

She wrinkled her nose and smiled at the same time. "See for yourself."

As expected, the deceased turned out to be a collection of alcoholic beverages. A box of Corona, two bottles of Chilean wine, and assorted heavier spirits.

"I was trying to get rid of that, so the boat wouldn't stink in the morning."

"Oh…"

"Well, you found it, you keep it. Why don't you give some to your buddies back there?"

"Wise girl." He grinned, left the wine bottles on a table and took the bag to the back of the cabin.

Beside the kitchen and bathroom, there was a mudroom, which now had the deflated rubber boat, plus air compressor and generator. By the far wall, there was a back room, home of the water tanks and the solar panels' management system. Nothing of it could be seen from the front of the cabin thanks to a dividing wall, which didn't reach the arched ceiling.

All his men had arrived and were setting up camp. The hammocks were already hanging from hooks on the walls, a folding table and chairs dominated the center of the room with a deck of cards already resting on top, and their bags were piled against the water tanks. Illumination was a lot better than on the main room. Under the fluorescent lamps, he could see the raw construction of the building, which was repurposed discarded tires filled with dirt and covered in cement.

"All set?" Hack asked.

"Yes," answered Renton. "Doors and windows secured."

"A present from the boat to ease the wait, gentlemen. Just remember you're still on duty."

Renton's mouth stretched, and his men looked at the bag with interest.

"Understood," he answered.

Hack nodded and headed back to see what the girl was doing. The room was in penumbra. Only two salt lamps glowed in the reigning darkness.

She had taken her sandals off and had climbed onto the bed to look out the window. Well, not exactly the window, but the slit they had left uncovered to check on the weather.

"Impressive," he murmured, looking at the twisting clouds and the swinging palm trees. Big waves crested in white foam smashed on the sand and retreated, only to try again, restlessly. Thunder boomed right after twisted fingers of light hit the ocean in the distance.

"Breathtaking. How can something so scary be so beautiful?"

"Nature can't help being beautiful. Not even when she is enraged."

Hack paused. He didn't sound like his old self at all.

His expert hands opened the wine bottle and served two glasses.

"Cheers for safety and a bright day tomorrow." They clank the glasses and tasted the wine. It was good, light on the palate with cherry and coffee tones in the aftertaste.

Her eyes were glowing when he deposited both glasses on a side table. She was both enthralling and enthralled. *She said she didn't want, but…*

He caressed her cheek with the back of his hand, and she leaned onto it, her eyelids half closed. Encouraged by her surrender, both hands covered the sides of her jaw and slowly brought his mouth to her.

Her lips, smooth and soft, opened effortlessly to his kiss. He didn't probe deep. His tongue just played, hoping to whet her appetite for more. Her compliance was precious and fragile. He wanted to take her slowly, go only as far as she was deeply comfortable with and, if she let him, give her a sweet, life-long memory. Her head fell back in surrender. He'd never experienced this with a woman: that feeling of full trust. It made him want to cherish and protect her, to hug her tight and never let her go.

Outside, rain and sand flew in the boisterous wind, making the world a hostile place and pushing them into each other's arms.

Without breaking the kiss, he laid her on his bed. Her hands were on his neck and her shoulders touched him oh so lightly. It drove him crazy. A clear order given from his groin to his brain: *time to plunge.* He resisted and didn't speed up. He wanted her to want him to the point of demanding it. He wanted her pulling at his hair and biting his shoulder. Asking him to go harder, asking him to go deeper.

Oh shit.

Like a bucket of icy water, realization dawned on him… he didn't have condoms. He did have some, but not the right ones. They were small, thick and with no lubrication whatsoever—the best for the survival kit, to gather water and make tourniquets. Definitely not for sex.

Well. This will take going slow to the next level.

He looked into her eyes. The magic was fading fast. She was rolling her eyes all around her, trying to figure out how she got to be lying down on his bed. He placed himself by her side and petted her arm with his palm.

"You... don't... want?" Her eyes were glossy.

"Oh I do, sweetheart. You have no idea how much..." he breathed, imprinting his words with all the meaning they really had.

Her mouth drew a coquette smile.

"But...?" she left the question open.

Hack felt like the biggest ass in the world. This had not been designed as a sex vacation. Bad, bad boy-scout... how humiliating. Humbling, really humbling.

"I have no condoms."

"Oh..."

"It doesn't matter," he added fast.

Her eyes opened like saucers and her eyebrows shot up. *Way to go, Romeo.* He had just killed all the magic left.

He had to act fast, without scaring her. If she got up, any chance of spending the rest of the day in her arms was gone. She seemed to have made up her mind since yesterday and was willing to try, but she could change again and decide otherwise.

"See this?" He touched the top of his swim pants. "It stays."

"Then..." She shook her head.

"Today it stays, and we make it all about knowing each other, and especially you. Tomorrow... I go to town and buy a twelve-count box."

Chuckling, she turned her face, hiding against his chest. That was a sweet lady.

"I have some..." she whispered oh so low he almost didn't hear.

It gave him pause. Really gave him pause.

"You do?" He put his finger under her chin to lift her face, but she resisted. The girl was trembling like a leaf. Either she was a gold medal con artist, or this was a true miracle.

"Show me," he encouraged her.

Hack suppressed the surfacing current of emotions, the ones doubting her being as innocent as he'd thought. He had no claim over her, and the way she had enjoyed her own body to that point was none of his business. Yet a man was a man, and he was a man through and through. Wanting to be special for a woman he cared about and not part of a laundry list was in his DNA. He *really* cared for her… *when did this happen?*

"Marita put them with my towels before leaving. One of her practical jokes."

He felt relief expanding in his chest. *Fuck political correctness. A man is a man.* Hack defended his emotions from his own punishing thoughts before they even emerged.

"With the towels? Let's see…"

He turned swiftly and left the bed, striding toward her bags and bringing the one with towels.

She knelt on the bed and retrieved a three-count package, giving it to him. He never used these because of the numbing shit in them, but the condoms were large, thin and lubricated. *Good enough.*

Outside, the wind had unrooted a palm tree and seemed determined to go for more. The noise of the falling tree shocked him to his core, and an urgent feeling hissed in the air between them.

Something primal came to him with the noise. The fear of death pushing them into each other's arms. Her eyes showed exactly the same primal need. Or not exactly. Her instincts were rocketing for to a lot more than fucking. She was primed to create life.

He kissed her again. There were no games this time. His tongue plunged into her mouth and she responded in kind. Taking him in like a silk cloth, she embraced his need with one of her own.

Her hands fisted his hair. *That's how I like it.*

Her tongue decided to come out to play, and they dueled and mated in a mimicked version of what was about to come.

Hack lifted her dress and his fingers dug into her buttocks. Ever since the day at the cave, he'd been hungering to do it again. She had a nice guitar shape, with small breasts and a very plump and sexy ass.

His hand slid down her thigh, looking for the ticklish point behind the knee. She rewarded him with a small jolt and kissed him even harder. He pressed her knee with one hand and squeezed her buttocks with the other. She understood right away and straddled him, giving the first attention to his already engorged rod. *Fuck, she feels so good.*

His hands slid up to take her dress off.

Then he felt it. *Sand.*

* * *

Yani

Yani felt the feathery touch on her leg and knew what it was right away. *Sand.*

It was too much. What else could go wrong? Right at that moment, lightening shook the earth and let her know how lucky they actually were and how fleeting life was.

Laughter took over. It was a nervous giggle at the beginning, but when she saw the humor in his eyes, it evolved into a full-bellied, boisterous laugh that embraced them both.

He hugged her tightly before standing with her still in his arms and placing her on the bed as if she weighed nothing.

"Please have a look at the condoms. See if the lubricant is water or oil based. I'll prepare the shower."

She nodded and reached for the condoms. It felt really good to be with someone like him. Decisive and intense, but with a great sense of humor. Someone who took problems in a stride without making a big deal of anything. It didn't hurt he had great pecs to rest her face on and strong arms to hold her.

"Shower ready," he simply stated when he came back.

"Water-based," she answered following his lead.

"Then leave it for later."

Why?

"The lubricant dilutes in water," he said, answering the question in her eyes.

He held his hand to her, and she took it without hesitation. Flings could be a really bad idea, but she was beyond caring.

The door to the mud room was closed and the bathroom smelled as if it had just been cleaned. She cherished the detail. A man who cooked for you could be fun, but a man who cleaned the bathroom for you… that was a knight in shiny armor.

He closed the door behind them and locked it.

Yani sensed his desire coming in waves of pleasure and anticipation. It made her feel powerful in a meaningful way, a private way.

She locked her eyes on his and removed the robe.

"More…" he whispered, and she took off her bikini in two swift movements.

He closed his eyelids half-mast and took a deep breath as if he were pulling her image in. She felt the most beautiful woman in the world.

Yani entered the shower. "Coming?" she said and didn't need to ask twice.

In thirty seconds flat, he had removed his swim trunks and had her pressed on the wall with his massive body covering her small frame.

His hands were everywhere. They roamed free, not stopping too long in any place, leaving her wanting. They caressed and squeezed while his mouth assaulted hers fiercely. His knees were bent, and his thick rod was trapped between their bodies. He pushed his hips forward and she squirmed, cutting the kiss. Pain had a sobering effect on her, and he had just stabbed her pubic bone.

He pulled back.

"You ok? Did I hurt you?"

Yani shook her head. "It's nothing." She kissed him, trying to start again.

He kissed her back and put some distance again, looking deep into her eyes.

"Turn around," he commanded.

Once obliging, he pressed himself against her cushy backside, and this time it didn't hurt one bit. It felt hot, oh *so hot*.

His mouth closed on her neck while his hands found her breasts. His hips started a rhythmic dance, that made her want to go wild and have him inside.

Her hips moved in circles, and he grunted in her ear while his right hand started to crawl down slowly, letting her know what he intended, making her want it.

His fingers found her apex and played with her curls. Her legs opened of their own accord. The fingers of his left hand squeezed her nipple at the same time that the index of his right hand found her clit. This time, the pain didn't hurt. It took her higher than ever before. She could feel her lower belly becoming heavy, and her folds pulsing in response to his hands.

Her hips followed an ancient choreography, she neither directed nor controlled. He growled in her ear and bit down on her shoulder while his right hand played her pussy like a piano. His fingers never stopping, his hips never stopping.

She lost all sense of time. She only knew that each time she felt she had enough, that the sensations where too intense, that she couldn't take it anymore… he doubled down and kept pushing her over the edge.

Electricity shot down her legs and she froze. Her head turned.

"I think I'm done." She was in awe.

His lips drew an imp grin and his hand squeezed her vulva. Another discharge of electricity shocked her.

"Not yet, but we're getting closer." The murmur sounded like a promise.

He kissed her, plunging her mouth with his tongue and doubled down, yet again.

Outside, the storm was in full strength, and inside her body, her soul felt pushed by similar energies. Pressure built in her belly in ways she never thought possible. She surrendered to the sensations, to his hands, to him…

"Come for me," he breathed in her mouth and plunged two fingers inside her. She screamed. Her vulva had come to life and was beating like a heart. She was lost in waves of intensity, as if lightening of her own making was running free right inside her.

She lost sense of place and time.

She felt how his strong arms picked her up and moved her. She heard a curse and something about sand. She felt she was sitting on him, and his rod entering her pussy from behind in one push. It felt tight, it hurt, and her spine bowed, bringing her back from her slumber.

"Shit! I'm sorry. Please tell me you're not a virgin."

"I'm not," she said, and smiled. It was the first time that her lost virginity was a good thing. She realized she was a woman, not a girl, and it felt just right.

He breathed heavily into her hair, and she moved her hips to encourage him. She was not hurt. She was alright. She was more than alright.

He growled and dug his fingers on her hips while his rod entered her fast and furious.

She relaxed and let him take his share with abandon. Behind her, he growled and cursed and pushed, and she rode it all, feeling happy and powerful, having her second peak just before he did.

He came grunting and held her, petting her hair for over five minutes before suggesting another shower.

Chapter 11

Yani

"Alright, girly. Time to talk." Marita was serious now, all determination and wild hair.

"Time to go back?" Yani sighed.

"Yes. At least we have to."

The boat had weathered the storm with dignity, but it had suffered, so they had no other choice than to take it to the local shipyard for the basic repairs and head back south. This meant that Yani's hideout was already gone. She would have to start moving, because someone could recognize her any minute.

Yani only wished she'd had time to say goodbye properly to the man who had changed her in the best possible way.

The day had stretched into the night, and they'd spent all the time in each other's arms. It had been the most magical day of her life. And the most fleeting one. She entered that hut thinking of herself as a girl, and left feeling like a woman.

In the morning Marita and Enrique had arrived, and mayhem burst forth. They checked the boat. They made decisions. The anchor lifted and she saw his image becoming smaller in the distance, without even a goodbye kiss.

"The question is: what are you going to do?"

"I don't know…"

"Not good enough, sister. You had plenty of time to think this past week. Tell me: what is that you want the most? Besides *Hot Hunk*, I mean..."

Yani smiled. Hut Hunk certainly suited him, a lot more than William. *Back to reality.*

"Hmm... I would like to be free from my father, and Marcos, and the drama. I would like to be normal."

"Good luck with that," Enrique interjected under his breath. He had followed Marita's instructions about Yani to the letter, and in his world, that meant almost not talking to her. But this time, as captain of the ship, he was here.

"Enrique..." Marita warned him.

"You got it wrong, sweetheart. Relax. I just meant that normal people are not free either. But, if what you want is to get away from the dicks in your life, then cross the border and go visit Uncle Sam. Experiment with the life of normal people. Then you'll have the tools to know what you want."

"I can't. The moment I show the passport, my father will know, and maybe Marcos too."

"And what if you don't have to show your passport?" Enrique asked.

"How? Oh no... I'm not walking. Are you crazy? The Devil's highway is even more dangerous than my father and Marcos put together."

"That's true..." Enrique said, scratching his stubble.

"What side are you on?" Marita smacked his shoulder and he grinned.

"Thank you," he answered, and Marita opened her eyes wide like plates.

"Oh no..."

"You know the rules..." he said, still smiling.

"Look, guys, do you need a moment?" Yani interjected sharply. Their sexual games permeated all aspects of their lives, and right at this moment, when she had found and lost love, when her life was at stake... it was too much.

"Sorry. You're right. We can leave the smacking conversation for another time."

Both girls gaped, and he went on as if nothing had happened. "I have a cousin who crossed the border. One baron put the death sign on him because he slept with his sister and never called her again. He crossed with a coyote that knows his business, and he delivered him to Florida, in a safe haven far from the crowded areas."

"Oh…"

"Don't get me wrong. It's shitty life. He works like an animal and just gets by. US allows illegals in only for slave labor, like all empires before it."

"That sounds very promising…" Marita muttered.

"Honestly, I don't know if you have what it takes to survive as a normal person. You're sweet and all, but let's face it, you're a spoiled brat."

"I beg your pardon?" Yani squared her shoulders and lifted her chin defiantly.

"It's not your fault. It's by design, I think, so you can never break free."

"Enrique, you are the biggest dickhead among the biggest dickheads. How can you talk to her like that?"

"You don't get it, do you, sweetheart? There are not ideal or easy ways available to her at this time, and we can spend the rest of our lives bringing ideas for her to reject as not good enough. What she wants is out of reach. She has to compromise and see what part of her life she is willing to sacrifice in order to save the rest. And if she doesn't choose, others will do it for her, as it's happened before."

"Enrique…" Marita warned him, but Yani stopped her.

"Wait. Thanks, Enrique, I think you're right. I have used my work as a way to run away and hide from life. That was my ideal, yet I traded one prison for another. And funny enough, I don't miss my job one bit. All what I thought was important, wasn't…"

Yani bit her lower lip and looked at the sky. She needed clear thinking at this time, but she was too distracted. She could still feel his hands on her skin, his lips on hers, and hear his grunts of pleasure. He was a gringo. What were the odds? *It's in God's hands.*

"You know what? I would like to go to the US. I know I don't want the other options, and my perfect little hideout from life is gone. Let's try something else, and if I can't take it, I'll call my dad... and if I die on the trip, well, maybe it would be for the best."

"Nothing better happen to her, or I'll hang you by the balls on the top of the mast." Marita stormed inside of the cabin, with tears in her eyes.

Enrique smiled with affection and pulled his cell phone. "Let me make some calls..."

Yani let her eyes drift in the horizon. *And if I die in the trip, maybe it is for the best...* Was she ready to die? She hoped she didn't have to find out.

* * *

The searing heat was like an iron mantle, pressing her down. The leather jacket Manuel, the coyote, had given her had done a great job during the cold of the night before, and to protect her from the thorny shrubs, but it was getting too heavy with her own sweat.

Her legs were wobbly, and her head light. She didn't know how much farther she was going to be able to walk.

Manuel came to her. "How are you holding up?"

"I wish I could say ok, but I'm not feeling well."

"Everyone stop!" Manuel said, low but emphatically.

"Manuel, this is not a good place, and you know it." One of his men came from the front and faced him. He had M13 tattooed on his neck and eyes that had seen death.

Manuel ignored him, took a blood pressure monitor out of who-knows-where and put it around her wrist. He sighed noisily and took a piece of translucent rock from his pocket.

"Lick it," he said.

"Excuse me?" Yani asked, disgusted.

"Girl, I'm not asking you to suck my dick. It's just salt. Now do it before you pass out, and we have to leave you to the vultures."

Yani's tongue was out before even thinking about it. The pungent flavor hit her taste buds and seemed to run through the roof of her mouth up to her head. It was a shocking sensation and pushed her upright with new alertness.

"Good," Manuel said. "Now drink."

He took her canteen and offered it. Yani's took it and drank greedily.

"What's your name?" He asked for the tenth time.

"Janice," she answered, alert.

"Good, good… we will not have to leave you here then." He patted her shoulder once and went towards his man.

Yani looked at him wide-eyed and had yet another epiphany during this trip. She was not ready to die after all…

Chapter 12

Hack

The long and black limousine stopped right in front of Hack and he entered without preambles. The men guarding his back didn't attempt to open the door for him. Those formalities would come when there was people watching. Here they were alone in the underground parking lot of his building, safe from prying eyes and stupid formality.

Rob was already inside the car, with a tux as elegant as Hack's own.

"Looking good, man," Rob said offering one of his signature smiles.

"Not bad yourself, either," Hack answered.

Rob scanned himself and pulled at the golden cuff-links of his shirt. "Did you arrange for your girl?"

"Hubert did. We sent her with your girl to the hotel to doll up."

"Thanks. Cynthia is going to love it."

Right at that moment, two members of his security team entered the limo and sat on the back seat. At the wheel it was Renton, his eyes alert in the rear mirror. Hack nodded once and the limo started its journey, a second car behind them.

The next stop was at the main door of a well known five stars hotel where Hack had hired two bedrooms to spend the night, and left their companions to use the premises and prepare for the gala.

Two beautiful women in their mid twenties entered the limo. The first was a redhead who seemed to have stepped straight out of a fairy world, the other one was an exotic beauty with raven hair and a lilting Asian ascent. The dress of this last girl was evidently haute couture, with sequin work that was art in its own right.

"I'm Paula," the dark haired said, as she sat by Hack's side.

"Pleased to meet you," Hack said. "I thought Sarah was coming tonight."

"She didn't pass the drugs test," Paula answered and made a tsk sound.

Hack shook his head. It was sad. The life of a escort as such was short. Sometimes they gained some cash and moved on, but too often it ended badly.

The other girl slid past them as best as she could and sat on Rob's lap at the end of the eight's passenger's limo.

"Hello Cynthia, you look stunning," said Rob in turn with his eyes sparkling in appreciation. "Are you ready for a night to remember?" he murmured in her ear.

Cynthia answered by placing his hand on her breast and nuzzling his neck.

Hack looked at Paula and they both chuckled. "So, you know the deal?" He asked businesslike.

"I'm escorting you to the gala. Need to look my best all the way through. No talking unless I'm addressed first. No providing personal information of any source. No drinking, just one flute of champagne for the whole night, no eating or doing anything improper."

"Perfect," he said and smiled.

"I'm here to serve," she answered and smiled seductively.

"Thanks, just hang on and we will have dinner when the gala ends."

"Thank you, but we already ate. You'll see two chicken salads with extra everything and grapefruit juice in the hotel slip. That was us. I hope it's ok?"

"Did the extra-everything include the dress?" Hack asked, his eyebrows slightly furrowed.

She chuckled. "Of course not. It's from an aspiring designer. Do you like it?"

"It's perfect," he said and smiled. "Did you have a massage?"

"I didn't know I could." Surprise opened her suggestive eyes.

"Now you do," he said.

"Now I see why Sarah and the girls were so eager over this assignment. They even considered rehabilitation to be ready for the next gala."

"Glad to hear." Hack grinned and she smiled back.

This girl was different. She didn't look like a regular escort. She seemed to have a clever head on her shoulders and didn't use heavy cake make-up to cover eye bags and other marks. Her skin was flawless. She was attractive, petite as he liked them, with a beautiful heart shaped face and shiny silky hair. A bit too slim, but good enough. If she wasn't an escort he might even be interested in knowing her better. *Maybe, maybe not.* Right at that moment the image of another petite and beautiful woman came to him, and he felt the pain of loss right in the middle of his chest. The girl of the boat had followed him into his dreams, entered his lonely hours, and apparently was determined to intrude into this gala as well. He hadn't had sex since the cove. Three weeks wasn't that much, was it?

Until the moment they arrived at their table, Hack had his best intention set in having a good time, even if the gala was just a way to funnel his hard earned cash to a far away cause. Sadly the cause would see just a fraction of his money after the organizers took their share.

Seated at their table was Millicent Pearson, a woman he'd crossed several times before in business training sessions. She was a crazy bitch and she was looking right into Rob's eyes with lascivious pleasure. Hack observed Rob, then worried. They had history, and not a nice one. His friend's face had blanched and he'd stopped breathing completely. It was as if he'd seen a ghost.

"Man, I can't go there," Rob said.

"I know," Hack answered. He didn't feel like going either. That woman was bad news. Whoever had set the positions at the table would hear from him. He turned and addressed his bodyguard. "Mr Renton, we are cutting the night short. Let's get out of here."

"Understood," Renton said and spoke into his mic. "One, bring the limo to the front, two and three, take positions. Four, get the second car ready. We are leaving."When Hack entered the limo, the image he saw was strange. Rob was hugging Cynthia, who wept silently. Their eyes met and Rob nodded. "I'm alright," he murmured. Hack jerked his head toward Cynthia. Rob sighed as response.

"What happened?" Paula asked once the car started again.

"I'm sorry, change of plans," Hack told her. "We will take you back to the hotel, and you have the night free. Take a massage. Enjoy yourself. Just don't bring anyone else."

"You are not coming?" She looked puzzled.

"Not tonight." Hack wasn't in the mood of having company. He took pride in making his companions enjoy themselves and most escorts had very hard shells. The first night was always challenging. From here, he just wanted to have a drink and go to bed.

"But we haven't talked about my dress yet."

"What about it?" *The dress?*

"I made it… I was wondering if you could sell it at your store…"

Holy shit. "Oh… so you are a designer besides an escort?"

She chuckled and shook her head. "There are no escorts clean of drugs… this new condition of you was impossible to meet in the agency. I'm not an escort, I'm Sarah's roommate. You are a difficult man to meet so I took this opportunity. She said I could say no and you would accept it, and that you were always willing to do business."

Hack tilted his head and assessed her all over again. "I love the dress, let me see what I can do." He pulled his phone and took a picture of her, sending it. "Lisa, meet Paula. She is a couture designer. Please make some time for her Monday morning. Thanks." He touched the screen and sent the voice message.

She curved a thin eyebrow at him. He took a card, wrote something on it and gave it to her.

"Go to this address, Monday 10:30 am, ask for Lisa. Take a presentation, and all the clothes you can show."

"All of them?"

"Yes. If your clothes meet our basic requirements, Lisa will help you grow from where you are to where we need you to be taken as an affiliate. She is great."

"I don't know how to thank you..." she said with tears in her eyes.

"Start by staying away from guys like me. Don't believe the glitter. Most won't take no for an answer, and what they ask for might not be simple vanilla sex. You get me?"

She nodded several times. "Ok..."

Chapter 13

Yani

Arms crossed in front of her body and slightly pouting, Yani watched in contempt as the cashier put item by item in the bags. The amount of unnecessary products Fabiane bought was increasing over time, and she was paying for half of them. Of course she loved Chilean wine, and Swiss chocolate, who didn't? Only that with her present job as a babysitting helper wannabe, she couldn't afford them and wouldn't have bought them. She didn't understand why Enrique had arranged for her to live with this woman at her arrival to the US. Yani had been delivered right by her doorstep without any discussion.

Since she arrived in Florida a month before she had been cleaning babies butts and puke ten hours a day, plus helping with cleaning, cooking and groceries. She loved cooking, and she also discovered she really loved children, but she definitely didn't love feeling she was living in semi-slavery. Not only had she received a flat salary that was ludicrous, she also had to pay for half the expenses and had no say in what to buy. She didn't have days off, nor was she allowed to go out on her own. Fabiane was clearly taking advantage of her, and her patience was running short.

"Are you going to put the bags in the cart or what?" Fabiane barked.

Yani'd thought Brazilians were cheerful and easy going people. Fabiane showed this part with her customers, but she was a tyrant.

Especially in public places, she seemed to thoroughly enjoy treating Yani like trash, showing who's boss so to speak.

"Coming," Yani muttered and obliged.

"Take this to the van and come back," Fabiane said and handled her the keys, once the first cart was filled to the top. They would probably need three carts, so it made sense.

Yani's steps dragged across the pavement. She hated to be like this. All her life she had been an overachiever, but the feeling of being abused and overworked made her bounce to the opposite side of the spectrum. She found herself cutting corners, what she'd never done in her entire life. Staying with Fabiane was destroying her from the inside out.

She put the groceries in the van, and took out her phone. "Just a bit of fun before facing the witch again," she muttered while typing the web address of her favorite store, HHLLC. She had just received her new credit card under the fantasy name Janice Simpson, which matched her fake driving license and social security number. So now she could actually buy books again. Maybe life would get better, or at least she could find a corner in the closet where the toddlers slept at nap time and hide.

Scrolling down to the bottom, she searched for a registration channel and found it right under a message that read: "We are hiring". Yani clicked on the link and found the offered positions. Most asked for experience, many she could have covered, but not as Janice Simpson. About half way down she found a position for data entry, no experience required. That could actually work. She looked into the details, *New York, he did speak fast, maybe he was from the Big Apple. What are the odds? Crazy small. So what? Can't be worst than this...*

An idea forming by itself in the back of her mind, Yani walked back into the mall. Fabiane was waiting for her with two carts ready to be taken to the van and back to the two bedroom apartment they shared.

"I forgot the cotton swabs," Fabiane said. "Wait here."

"Ok," Yani answered.

When the woman went back into the maze that was the store, Yani felt it was now or never.

"Can you look after the carts for my friend and give her these when she comes back?" she gave the keys of the van to the cashier. "I need to use the restrooms real quick and don't want to leave her waiting."

"Sure," the lady said and gave her a knowing smile.

Yani ran toward the bathroom, only to go on and leave the store through the furthest door, the one that went to the garden products' area.

"Now what?"

She had her phone, her credit card and her IDs in a small purse, and the clothes she had on. That's it. Those were her sole possessions if she chose to go through with her plan.

She walked briskly toward the closest avenue and stopped a cab.

"Deerfield Beach train station," she said.

The man nodded and put the car in gear.

Chapter 14

Hack

Hack woke up in a puddle. This new, healthy lifestyle was getting on his nerves. Being a horny teenager all over again at almost forty was not what he had envisioned. His long fingers pulled the covers off, showing his naked body. *Morning wood on top of it, just what I needed.*

While the cold water filled up the tub, he poured in some ice cubes and dove in. Cold water baths were another recommendation of Dr. Quack. It was absolutely crazy—like using only soft orange light at night, eliminating WiFi completely, sleeping on a magnetic mattress and being in bed by nine—but he had to admit he hadn't felt sharper in years. And the Himalayan salt lamps gave his high tech place a homey feeling. Problem was, he woke up hornier than ever and using escorts was out of the equation for now. Hubert was right. Addictions were a door to danger he didn't want to be close to.

"The solution is simple. Get a wife," Dr. Quack had said when he complained about his predicament. "Why do you think married men live longer and happier lives? Their basic needs are covered. Diversity is good for a time, but it gets old too."

The man was definitely a loony, but a highly efficient one.

While the cold engulfed him, he thought about the girl on the boat, yet again. She had blossomed right in front of his eyes into the sweetest, funniest, strongest, hottest and most caring woman he'd ever encountered. His male pride had taken charge when he realized she was climaxing in his arms for the first time, and he'd decided to give her a day to remember. It had backfired though, as now he was the one who couldn't get over her. His dick twitched in spite of the cold. *You miss her too, hum?*

His mind fished for a practical solution to his predicament. How about the brunette? She hadn't shown any interest in him as a man. It'd been just business. Would she sleep with him? *Possibly.* Would he sleep with her? *Maybe.* Would he date her? *No.* Would she accept a non strings attached relationship? *Possibly, but not for long.* Hack sighed and dipped his head under the frozen water.

Man, you are screwed.

* * *

"News?" Hack asked, entering the monitor room. Hubert Wilson, his head of security, lifted his eyes from the paperwork he was reviewing.

"There is a possible problem. Still not sure it's worth your time."

"Tell me about it," the tall man took a chair across from him, putting his arms on its back.

Wilson looked amused. "Bored?"

"Annoyed."

"Oh. Alright. Here's our problem." Hubert passed his boss the picture of a woman.

Hack's jaw dropped.

"Pretty, hmm?"

"Yes," he managed to answer, still in shock. "What about her?"

"She's too good to be true, and she doesn't exist."

"Tell me the tale."

"She applied for data entry. Her IQ is one hundred and twenty five. She had zero errors entering data on the three runs. The third one was in French and she used the accent alt keys with no hesitation whatsoever. Oh, and her speed is eighty words a minute."

"So we have an overqualified applicant," Hack followed the reasoning, but his eyes were glued to the image.

"A ghostly overqualified applicant…"

"Hum?"

"Her background check came empty—not even a parking ticket—and her credit score is zero."

"Valid SSN?"

"Yes."

"Valid address and phone number?"

"Yes."

"Drug check?"

"Squeaky clean."

"Does she have a faint New England accent? Like if she'd gone to Yale?"

Wilson's eyebrows shot up. "How did you know?"

"Hire her."

"She could be a spy."

"Keep an eye on her then."

"You're the boss. But what if she's a spy?"

"Might be, but I think not. I think she's undocumented."

"We never hire illegals. Your rules…"

"I know. But you said it, she is not just any illegal. And she has an SSN, so we can play dumb and get away with it. What's her name?"

"Janice Simpson. You know this girl, don't you?"

"I'm keeping this," Hack answered, showing the picture.

The girl from the boat smiled awkwardly back at him from the image. She had square librarian glasses and her hair up. But it was definitely her.

Chapter 15

Yani

Yani paid her ticket and went right to gallery 818, one of the three main rooms in the Met that held French Impressionist painters. She felt before seeing the image she was looking for. *Jardin à Sainte-Adresse* had caught her heart many years back in her first trip to the States, when her mother herded her to the Art Institute of Chicago to see a Monet exhibition. It was love at first sight. She didn't know why, and she didn't care. This wasn't the most acclaimed painting by Monet, but it talked to her inner child about home and family, and pretty flowers and the promise of an ocean splash. It made her heart sing.

Today she was celebrating and decided to do it her way. A visit to the museum, lunch at Loeb's with a gorgeous view to the lake in Central Park and then a visit to Raaka for a decadent virgin chocolate bar.

She had a job. One she found all by herself. One that was not flashy, but it was something she was able to do with ease. It didn't fully cover her expenses, but she had managed to move money using bitcoins to her new account so she had some leverage. Being careful, she could keep this going for several years before asking for help. Good enough.

Here she was, watching at the sailboats rock on the silvery water, in front of the best meal she had eaten in a long time, and still keeping fresh the memory of her favorite painting. Living life in her own terms for the first time ever. *Exhilarating.*

* * *

Her feet killing her, Yani plopped on her bed/couch and sighed with contentment, looking at the small box of chocolate in front of her.

She had a place, she had a job and most importantly: she had peace. What she didn't have was a maid...

"Alright, girl. Get up. You are not in Cartagena. There're no magic hands in this house and you start working tomorrow. But first..." Kicking her shoes off, she crossed one leg over the other, closed her eyes and rubbed the arch of her foot. "Mmm that feels so good, don't stop." A smirk curved her mouth and her eyes flew open. She wiggled her toes, inspecting them.

"Sure, like Mr. Hot Hunk will arrive in his shiny armor to rub my sore feet anytime soon. I wonder where he is..."

Probably with wife and kids in some mansion. *No.* He didn't have a ring and he'd said he slept with prostitutes, while fending off money groupies.

I miss you.

After taking the thin stockings off and massaging both feet, she felt almost human again.

Then it was time to go out onto the balcony and water her plants. She'd been in that apartment less than a month and it was already crowded. Her blueberry bush was full of ripe fruit. "Mmm! A special treat for later."

Dancing at the rhythm of "El Amor de mi Tierra," by Carlos Vives, her curves waved around, while expert hands organized the house. She thoroughly cleaned the bathroom and vacuumed the floors, even though they were still clean from the day before.

Yani was happy being Janice. Stripping all the glitter, fear and pain from her life allowed her to see deeper. Now she had the time and freedom to explore her inner self, to get to know the woman she'd become while running in circles, too busy to pay attention. It was liberating, an adventure in itself. The only thing she regretted was to have parted ways with the hottest, most caring, funniest guy on earth without even a goodbye kiss, or at least a phone number, or a name for that matter.

And now she was hooked ... to a memory.

Mmm speaking of which... the best part of the day: shower with Mr. Hot Hunk.

Janice took her glasses off, let her hair down and looked forward seductively, unbuttoning her blouse slowly. *Do you like what you see?* Her imaginary lover of course said *yes* and started the sensual ritual which had become her shower.

Yani walked to the bathroom, both hands on her breasts. She swayed her hips as if her man was walking just behind her, watching her sinuous movements. She could feel his need, and she enjoyed giving him a view. Her own need rose. Her skin became more sensitive, and she could feel the caress of the air as if it were his hands, his skin.

She stepped into the steaming water and his hands were everywhere. She let the water run over the nape of her neck, where she had that spot that made her feel cherished. The water ran down her back and the curve of her buttocks, down her legs. She was being thoroughly touched and prepared for what would come. Yani put her face under the water now, and it ran down her front. He was behind her now. He felt just perfect.

He purred in her ear, *I want you*, and she answered, *you have me*. He found the right spot between her legs and her pelvis danced. It was him on her back, inside her, while his hand worked her need. It was him raining kisses on her shoulders. Her movements became more erratic, and the pressure on her lower belly became unbearable. She persevered. She needed relief. And it came, small waves of pleasure pulsing in her lower belly, starting right were her hand was and running down her legs.

She let her head fall against the wall on top of her palm so she could catch her breath. She felt sated, satisfied.

Yet, deep down, there was a hint of sadness and grief. This was nothing like the day they spent together. He had ruined her for a long, long time.

Chapter 16

Hack

"Here, boss. Delivery." Hubert Wilson placed a package with a dozen frozen plastic jars over the mahogany desk.

"Thanks, man. You are a lifesaver. Let's go upstairs and eat. And what's over there?" Hack signaled a single package tied with a ribbon.

"Oh, that's from our spy girl. She's buying my silence with home-made blueberry pie. And let me tell you something: it's working. I saw her eating yesterday, asked for a piece, and she brought me a whole one. I'm lovin this assignment!"

"Darn. Grains and sugar are off the diet."

"Good. More for me." The old man grinned. "You should still try it, and, I don't know, drop by and thank her..."

Hack sighed. One of these days he would find a way to *thank her.* He had fantasized many times about how he would do it. Over his desk, arms and legs spread, her soft breasts on the wood, and her perfect perky ass in the air. Or in his chair, her back to him while he fucked her brains out. Or, his favorite, against the wall, her legs around his waist and his tongue ramming into her mouth in perfect synchronization with his dick in her pussy. Oh yeah, he had to thank her properly, *pronto.*

They walked toward the private elevator that led to his penthouse. Saying that he practically lived in his office was an understatement.

"Tell me again why we can't just use the microwave to heat these," Hubert asked, wrestling the frozen cubes into a cast iron pot.

"The radiation is toxic, or that is what Doc. Quack said."

The old man chuckled. "You keep calling that witch doctor names, yet you follow his crazy instructions to the letter."

"I'm conflicted about it, ok? But if I can hold off the heart attack while keeping my balls, I will."

They sat at the kitchen table and ate in silence.

He *had* to drop by. He couldn't keep stalking her through the security system anymore. The woman was turning him into a freakin' psycho.

* * *

This is a bad idea. Hack's fingers racked his hair. His reflection in the rounded mirror of his office's bathroom looked pretty good, actually. Nice bronze tan and golden streaks on his chocolate hair were new acquisitions. A smooth shave and deep blue eyes were his signature mark. *I look like a fucking surfer.*

His mouth quirked into a smirk. The humor of his own stupid objections didn't escape the fine-tuned machinery that was his brain. The girl had been working at H.H. LLC for a full month now, and she was becoming a permanent fixture in his office. That is, the camera showing Janice Simpson working at her desk was a permanent fixture. The woman... didn't even know he was around.

He couldn't go on like this. He needed some kind of closure for a relationship that never was and maybe could never be. *Why the hell did I hire her? Now I can be sued for even thinking about her.* And he was thinking about her alright, naked and practicing the whole set of Kama Sutra positions on his bed one by one.

With a last tightening of the necktie, he headed to the elevator. Destination: second floor.

Clearing his throat didn't work. Janice had a headset on, and Enya's "Only Time" floated softly around her. But it did call the attention of the other six people who were at the office.

"Miss Simpson?"

Startled eyes shot up and zeroed on his. Her mouth rounded in a spooked *Oh*. Two hands went slowly to the headset and removed it.

"What are you doing here?" Her eyes sparkled and a smile started to form.

"Em… Miss Simpson. I'm Hack Humphrey."

He offered his hand while his eyes rolled in circle to remind her they were not alone. Her eyebrows furrowed as her small palm fit into his. Like the first time they met, it felt more like holding than shaking. Warmth spread up his arm. It would be a nice moment, if Hack didn't feel also a dozen eyes darting his skull.

"Hack Humphrey? as in H. H. LLC?"

"Indeed. Um, your application was impressive. I just wanted to drop by and *welcome you aboard*."

A secretive smile pulled at the seam of her lips and her cheeks tinted a light shade of rose. "Thank you, *sir*. Highly appreciated."

"Right. Well." He let go of her hand and engaged their audience:

"I appreciate what each one of you is doing for the company. Thank you all. Miss Simpson." He nodded towards her.

"Thanks again for the warm welcome, sir." She nodded back.

With no more excuses to be there, Hack left the room feeling like he was in one of those dreams where you perform with no pants in front of a big audience. Well, at least it was done. Next time, he would call her to the tenth floor instead. If there was a next time…

Chapter 17

Yani

Yani's left hand picked up an apple, while her right one was entering data, her eyes never leaving the paper in front of her.

A full week had passed since that first encounter with her *boss*. And her emotions had been flipped upside down and inside out, never to calm down again. Her grief was replaced by hope, her peace by anxiety. Every day was excruciating. She wanted to run to him, but instead she just waited for his next move. He didn't come over again, even when she stayed late every day on purpose. He didn't call. Nothing. Maybe he was yet another case of initial interest followed by a monumental vanishing act. The story of her life. All her dates had followed that same pattern. Only that she hadn't had sex with any of them. If he wasn't interested, why did he come in the first place? And if he was interested, what was taking him so long?

A swishing sound startled her.

"It's late, Miss Simpson. You'd better leave now, or your man is going to storm the building," Hubert Wilson, the chief of security, joked. He was a lanky black man in his mid-sixties, with more salt than pepper hair, thinning at the top.

Janice chuckled. "Sure he will."

"You know, if I were thirty years younger, you would be my first choice."

"So you mean that I'm not a complete mess? Just was born at the wrong time?"

"You're not a mess. Period."

"Thanks, Mr. Wilson, you're very kind." She looked into the man's eyes and saw pity. She couldn't stand it. Her mouth pulled up in a fake smile. "I'm done. Thanks for taking care of me. I highly appreciate it." She slid up the bridge of her glasses to hide her glossy eyes.

Mr. Wilson smiled and moved a hand dismissively. "I'm not. I'm just doing my job. If your man comes storming in, I'll need to protect Mr. Humphrey's property, and there will be a fight."

Yani laughed again at the joke, but mostly did it to hide her emotions. Since a week ago, her ears felt hot when she heard that name.

The guy of the cove...

The guy that had walked at the beach with her talking about Gaudi, the Great Wall of China, and the magical system of the kahunas...

The guy that had protected her from a hurricane and had made love to her in the most sublime way...

The man that haunted her dreams and her fantasies...

...had turned out to be Hack Humphrey, her boss.

So close and so far away at the same time.

"Well, this is it. Thanks again. Have a good night." Nodding to Mr. Wilson, she headed to the door.

"It's really too late. Let me walk you to the bus stop," he offered.

Her defense systems went off, and her spine stiffened. "It's really not necessary, thank you."

"Alright," the man accepted, lifting both hands as a sign of surrender.

Yani walked the first block toward the bus stop looking over her shoulder. Mr. Wilson was following her at a distance, and it was seriously creeping her out.

She pressed on and walked faster. Her senses were wide open now. She felt the danger coming from her left before seeing the thug in the shadows. *Just in case.* Her legs sled sideways, taking her toward the edge of the street. There was a van parked just a few feet up front. Too close for comfort.

The man jumped over her when she was just a step from the curb. "Come here, sweets," he said with a gruff voice.

She ran, trying to cross the street, but he was faster. The man caught her arm and forced her to spin.

The spin made her face the path she had just walked. There was Mr. Wilson with his gun drawn and pointed at the confusing mass of bodies. He nodded at her and she let herself fall to the ground. The noise of fireworks exploded in the air, and her attacker growled, covering his hurt arm and letting go of her.

Yani crawled, and then ran away from her attacker and back to the safety Mr. Wilson offered. The creep disappeared into the shadows.

"Want me to hunt him down?" Wilson asked.

"No." Yani panted and braced her hands against her knees to catch her breath. "He looked like a creep after some cash."

"May I say: *I told you so?*" Wilson's face crumpled.

Janice giggled, still struggling to breath. "You may."

"Alright. Let me take you home."

Yani's eyebrows joined, her mouth putting slightly. "It's not necessary…"

"I insist."

"Look…"

"Sorry, darling. I know it freaks you out, but at this point that's the least of my concerns. My main concern is how I'm going to tell my boss that you were attacked."

"Hack? I mean, Mr. Humphrey?"

"The one and only."

When they were inside the car, Yani asked the question that was starting to burn the pit of her stomach. "Why did you follow me?""I had a hunch."

"Did Mr. Humphrey send you to watch after me?"

The old man grinned. "To keep an eye on you in case you are a spy. You are awfully overqualified, and we both know it."

"He thinks I'm a spy?" Her eyes couldn't get bigger if she tried.

Wilson laughed. "That's what I thought when I saw your application, and he ran with it. It's evident that you two know each other, but I'm too old to put my nose into stuff that's none of my business."

Wilson headed west toward her place, and they drove silently for about five minutes. "Want to grab something to eat?" he asked Yani when they approached a fast food place.

"No, thanks. I'll pass."

"Clever girl." The old man stopped by the mic and asked for a medium size grilled chicken sandwich and a salad. No fries or soda.

"Do you like that stuff?"

"I hate it. It's chemical warfare. But since my wife Lilly passed two years ago, I've got not much of a choice. I can take care of everything else, but her stews... those can't be bought."

He threw the package in the back of the car and took her home.

"You know," Yani said when they parked, "I cook big pots of stew and soup on the weekends, enough to last for the whole week. If you want, I can make double and we share."

His head slanted.

"Will you let me bring you home?"

"No."

"Then, thanks but no."

"Alright. I'll think about it..."

Hubert's grin went all the way up to his ears. "Darling, you got yourself a deal."

Chapter 18

Hack

Hack opened the door of the monitor room and caught his chief of security in the act. Hubert looked transfixed. He squinted and gazed under the table to see if there was someone there, because the man seemed to be having an orgasm.

But, no. He was eating soup.

Hack snatched the bowl and put a spoonful into his mouth. It was like nothing he had eaten before. It was not only the taste, rich and thick, it was the feeling of *coming home*, wherever that was.

Hubert growled and stood up.

"Where did you buy this?" Hack asked.

"Give it back. You're my boss, but you and I will brawl if you don't give me my soup back." The old man put his palm upwards and wiggled his fingers. Hack gave in grumpily.

"So, where did you buy it? I want some."

"You can't buy it. It's not for sale," the tall man said between spoonfuls, eating fast and almost choking.

"What do you mean it's not for sale?"

"Cub, you have a long way to go… the really important things in life don't have a price tag. This…" He drank the last drops right from the bowl and sighed, satisfied, "was given to me as a gift. It's distilled kindness. If you try to buy it, it won't taste the same."

Hack found Hubert's words exciting.

"Tell me the story."

"Why?"

"Just tell me the story."

"Alright. I was going to tell you anyway…" Hubert sighed, his expression soured. "There's this girl, what was her name? Oh yes… Janice Simpson, one of your data entry people."

The caught Hack's attention. Big time. The old man smirked.

"I've been keeping an eye on her because she's hiding something. I still don't know what it is, but I *will* find out."

His smirk grew even bigger, and Hack answered with a grin of his own.

"Last night I came here and saw Malcolm Stewart jerking off with his eyes glued on her monitor."

"What?" Hack's eyebrows knitted. Hubert's hand swiped an imaginary fly.

"It's usually nothing to worry too much about. People work too much, have no time for a life, and sex is a basic need. If it doesn't happen outside, it will happen inside.

"Anyway. Malcolm has a dark streak. He's too new to be breaking rules and I've got a soft spot for the girl. She tries so hard to hide that she just stands out."

"I noticed…"

"You noticed, hmm? You better hurry up. That fruit is ripe."

Wilson pointed at a monitor and there she was, working in one of the data-entry stations, in very proper clothes, cycglasses and a tight bun. She did look out of place in a beautiful-artwork-hung-askew sort of way. It was the same image that had haunted Hack for the last month.

"Well, I gave him two hundred bucks and laid him off. Told him to go get a pro and leave the girl alone."

"You did what?"

"Man, you really don't know what happens under your roof, do you? Let me spell it out for you. Do you think my job is to protect the building from robbery? Well, you're wrong. I work on *hump damage control.* You have no idea what I've caught on camera from the repository warehouse..."

"Really? I had no idea." Hack scratched his head.

"Now you do." He smiled sideways and continued. "Anyway, it was very late, about eight thirty, when the girl left the building. I went after her because... well, I don't know, I had a hunch. A block from here, Malcolm attacked her. I stepped in and he ran. She never saw him before and thought it was just a thug trying to take her purse. I know better." Hubert took a sharp intake of air and clenched his hands into fists.

"Where is he now?" Hack was ready to lift the man by the neck with one hand against the wall and give him a piece of his mind with his fist. *Nobody messed up with his woman.*

"He vanished. His place is empty, his car is sitting there abandoned, but he's nowhere to be found. I just sent an alert to motels and car rentals. Let's see what happens."

"Shit." Hack massaged his jaws with both hands. "Do you think she could be in danger? Do we appoint someone to her?"

"I really don't know. Normal people don't have bodyguards following them around. It would scare the crap out of her."

"I don't know. She seems ok with them..." Hack murmured. Hubert smirked, again.

"Anyway, I drove her home, and she pitied my food choices. So, today, she brought me *this little piece of Heaven,*" he stared wistfully at his empty bowl "and promised to do it every day. Man, I tell you. My Lilly's food was the best, but this one's even better. If I were thirty years younger, I would be down on one knee and proposing right now."

Hack's face crumpled, and the old man exploded in boisterous laughter. "Man, you are so screwed..."

The younger man lifted the right corner of his mouth, but his eyes became misty. No way to deny it. He certainly was. Now he only had to go down on one knee and propose?

Not that simple...

Chapter 19

Yani

The phone rang, startling Yani. She had lost track of time. Being a Friday night, the place was deserted. Her computer time read 7:12.

"Hello?"

"Janice? It's Hack Humphrey. Would you mind coming up to the tenth floor? I need to have a word with you."

Yani's hands started to shake.

"Of course. Right away."

Hot Hunk wanted her to go to the tenth floor. She had hoped for this, but now she was scared to death. He was her boss for goodness sake! She had put herself in this position by working late every night, and now she couldn't stop shaking. What did he want? She knew what she hoped he wanted. But here she was *Janice*, an illegal immigrant at the bottom of the barrel. Would he be her knight in shiny armor or a plantation master chasing after the new slave? Or maybe he would simply ask her to leave because she was too much trouble and wasn't worth the risk. None of that made sense. He had appointed Mr. Wilson to look after her. Yet… it had taken forever to call her. And then there was the episode the night before. She didn't feel safe anymore. She was seriously considering trying her odds in a small town in the middle of nowhere, a place in rural America where everybody knew everybody and there were no thugs in the streets. Did that place even exist?

Her legs seemed to have a mind of their own, she realized, when she pressed the button on the elevator but walked past it. At first, she thought she was going to the restrooms, to see if she was presentable, but they actually moved on toward the security room. *Mr. Wilson.* She had to tell him she was going upstairs, or he would be worried.

"Give me the key, old man, and I might let you live." The voice was loud and clear behind the closed door.

"Look, we have visitors," another guy said.

"She's mine," a third one growled, and she recognized the raspy tone of the man that had assaulted her the night before.

"Run! Fire!" Mr. Wilson yelled at the top of his lungs and Janice sprinted as if she were escaping from a stampede.

Fire, what did he mean? *Of course.* She opened the tiny glass door and pulled the handle to start the fire alarm.

Looking back, she saw two bulky men running after her. One was the creep from the street. She panicked, her hands shaking violently again. There was no way to muscle her way to safety, except... the elevator was right there, waiting for her.

She stormed inside and punched the tenth floor button.

Please, hurry! The door seemed to close slower than ever.

It locked just in time. She could hear curses on the other side. *What on earth have I gotten myself into?*

With her heart thumping in her chest, Yani looked at herself in the mirror. Her fear subsided, replaced by a different type of anxiety. Strands of hair had escaped from her bun and floated around her head. Her face had gone a ghostly chalk-white. The mascara was smeared, and the lipstick completely gone. She looked like a funny character in a Halloween movie. Pouting disapprovingly at her own reflection, she removed the pins and remade the bun, ironing the treacherous strands into place, before cleaning the black shadows under her eyes with her fingers from edge to edge, giving them a cat-like look. *Men are hunting you down and you're worried about your appearance? Way to go, girl.* She put hands on hips. *Well, creeps or not, I'm going to see Hot Hunk.*

She straightened her clothes and turned around to see if there was anything out of place.

She didn't want to think about the men, especially the one who had said she was *his*. She didn't want to connect these dots with her past either. Worrying about her looks was much easier and put her deeper fears at bay.

Everything came back when the doors opened. Hack was waiting for her on the other side of the elevator. "What happened?" he scowled.

"They have Mr. Wilson. Three men. I triggered the alarm and ran here. They're coming," Yani blurted.

The alarm noise stopped at that same moment. A second elevator was coming up and already on floor nine.

"Come with me," he commanded, taking her hand and striding into his office, straight to the furthest wall. Yani noticed the room was dark. Just a Himalayan salt lamp set in a corner and the computer screen pushed away the shadows. They reminded her of the day they spent in the cabin. *Not now.* An elevator slid open and he pushed her in, pressing one of the only three positions. The door opened almost right away into a huge apartment. The place was dark too; only a few salt lamps here and there. *He* had a thing for them, apparently.

One touch to the top molding of the elevator and the door grew bars—mean, thick ones—with almost no space in between. Yani didn't have much time to gawk, as he pulled her into one of the rooms. It was an office. Hack sat at his computer.

"C'mon, c'mon, c'mon," he muttered, moving the mouse back and forth.

The monitor flared to life revealing the arrow of a cursor. One click, and all the camera feeds in the building flashed onto the screen. But they showed no activity.

"He was in the security office?"

"Yes." She nodded.

The mouse clicked on a different icon and it showed another set of cameras. These had weird angles, and the images were not as clear.

Another click zoomed in on the security office. There was Mr. Wilson, unconscious, but still breathing.

"Sonofabitch!" His hands flew on the keyboard and many images came and went. Hack took a deep breath, sat back and looked at Yani.

She was staring blindly at the image of the old man on the floor. Hack put his hand over hers and she jumped, startled. His mouth curved in a crooked smile and he tried again. His finger moved forward and carefully grazed her arm, making Yani feel goose bumps in all the right places—or wrong ones, given the circumstances. Their eyes were locked now, and her breathing became shallow.

"It's alright," he said, massaging her arm up and down. His eyes were like magnets; she almost forgot what she wanted to say. Almost.

"No, it's not. Mr. Wilson is there. We need to do something." She pointed at the monitor.

He stood and cupped her face with long fingers, his other hand on her waist. His voice was soft and soothing.

"We're safe here. They can't reach us. I just shut down the whole network. Whatever they came for, they're not getting it." A big Cheshire cat grin spread across his face.

Yani snapped. The old man was hurting, and he was only worried about his own safety and the business. *Selfish son of a bitch.* "Didn't you hear me? Mr. Wilson is hurt. We need to help him!" Her finger stabbed the monitor.

Hack huffed, and she gave a step back. His eyes were stormy, and his lips pressed together.

"You don't understand. I pay him to keep *me* and *my business* safe. That's *his job.* And he's breathing. The backup team will be here any minute and they'll take these clowns down."

It was her turn to huff. But she might not be as impressive as he was, because he only arched one eyebrow and his lip twitched. Now, she was *really mad.*

"I understand, *sir,* that people are just *instruments* for you. But I live by a different set of *values.* Please open that door so I can go down and help Mr. Wilson."

His nostrils flared and his face settled into a scowl. She had managed to banish that smirk. *Good.*

"And what exactly are you going to do?"

"I don't know. Something, anything..." The impossible chasm between wanting and achieving dawned on her, but she didn't let it stop her. A friend needed help. She was going.

His eyes darted toward the monitor and came back to her.

"Do you think I don't care about him? He trained me in military school. He kicked my ass more times than I can remember, he also saved it once. He's like a father to me. I gave him this job as an *easy* retirement. He comes and goes as he pleases. He does whatever he wants. And you tell me I don't care?" his deep voice boomed.

"You care?" she asked levelly.

"Of course I do!" he answered. There was deep sorrow and anger in his eyes.

"Prove it!" Her jaw clenched and her finger pointed at the door.

"You don't understand. I. Can't. Go."

She put fists on hips. "Then. I'll. Go."

"Woman, you are impossible!" Hack stormed out of the office.

She followed his noisy footsteps and saw him putting a bulletproof vest on. He took two scary-looking knives from a cabinet in the wall and added a revolver. His hands expertly loaded the thing and stuffed his pockets with three additional clips. As an afterthought he also picked up a vile and a syringe.

He strode back and put a headset with an attached microphone around her neck. His brows were furrowed and his mouth, a thin line of contempt, but his hands worked gently.

"You stay here," he ordered. "You owe me for this. And if you come after me, I will spank you until my hand hurts. Get it?"

Yani's naughty side chose that moment to play tricks. *Is that a promise*, she heard in her mind. Her face turned completely red. He arched one brow and smiled sideways. Then shook his head and left through another elevator that was hidden in the wall, disguised as a mirror. The man had toys.

"Go to the computer," the sound of his voice was clear on the headset.

She ran back to the office and sat on the chair. "I'm here."

"Look into the guard room, is the old man alone? Click on the small icon of that camera to zoom in."

"No. There's a man with him," her voice trailed off.

"Talk to me."

"He is looking at the TV sets. One of the men is outside your office. I guess the other is inside."

She continued "I sort of know the man outside your office. He assaulted me last night a block from here. Mr. Wilson saved me."

"Holy shit," Hack murmured.

To her surprise, a panel opened behind the man in the guard's office, and Hack came out of it, silent as a shadow.

One hand had a knife and the other the syringe. The knifed arm strangled the man, the other hand puncture his neck with a mean needle, injecting him with something. Not an ounce of hesitation showed in his actions. The man fell to the floor almost immediately.

Hack picked up Mr. Wilson and slipped back through the open panel. It closed behind them as if no door was there.

Janice ran to the living room when she heard Hack grunting. He carefully lowered the old man from his shoulder onto the sofa and gave her a hard look.

"You haven't even kissed me today and I already took a man out for you," he scolded. "Woman, you are truly high maintenance. When Hubert wakes up, he's going to kick my ass."

Yani's face was ghostly white. "Did you kill him?"

"I hope not, or Hubert will kick my ass twice... it's horse anesthesia. He will wake up, eventually. Remember, you owe me a kiss," he admonished and strode to the furthest room down the hall.

Chapter 20

Hack

Once in the shower, Hack analyzed the situation. There were still intruders running rampant in his building and the security guards were probably out of business. Malcolm Stewart was one of them, and the bastard knew the place. He ground his teeth remembering Hubert's recollection of their last encounter. On the bright side, they were safe in the penthouse and the main information was out of reach. Where was Renton and the backup team? Why hadn't they responded to the fire alarm yet? They were the only reason he hadn't locked the building. *What a mess!*

As the hot water relaxed him and his lathered hands massaged his body, his thoughts moved from the intruders to the beautiful woman in his living room. Talking about timing… A smile spread across his lips remembering the sensations when they touched. *She's still mine.* When he said he'd spank her, her face became red as a strawberry, all the way to the ears. Did she like to be spanked? His dick twitched at the image of that delightful heart-shaped ass up in the air. How would it feel under his hand? He was not into that lifestyle, but domination techniques had been part of his business training. So if she wanted to explore her inner landscape, he could oblige. The girl seemed more on the vanilla side though, or maybe it was just hopeful thinking. Subs were too often emotional train-wrecks, and doms were out of the equation. He needed a sweet but strong woman by his side. One that blessed his heart and kicked his ass like only old-fashioned ladies could. Doctor's orders.

She was so close. How would it feel to have her in the shower with him again? He imagined ramming into her tight pussy from behind, her ass-cheeks slamming into him while he took her fast and hard. He hadn't been able to do that before. Fucking water-based lubed condoms.

Shit. He had the hell of a boner now.

By the time he finished dressing, his lust was fighting tooth and nail to take charge. He needed her, he wanted her, and he was going to have her, consequences be damned.

Once in the living room, the sight in front of him didn't help either. Janice was bent over, applying an ice pack to Hubert's head. A pang of anger hit his gut. He didn't want to share her. *Man, you are so screwed.* Perceiving that she was not alone, her head snaked around, and her eyes zeroed in on him.

"Are you all right?" she asked, worried.

"Yes, considering…"

"The man you took out?"

"He was trespassing and armed. The law is on my side," he responded more forcefully than he intended.

"I know. It's just… are you alright?"

Her concern cut through his thick skin. "I will be." A deep sigh escaped his chest. His lust had turned down its volume and blended with tenderness.

"So, where's my thank-you kiss?"

"Do you really want a kiss? Right now?"

"Yup." He signaled his cheek with a finger.

Janice smiled, shaking her head softly. "Alright." She moved closer and placed her cold hands on his neck, pulling him down. She planted a peck on his cheek as he had instructed, her eyes shining with expectation. She wanted more, and so did he.

Hack took her glasses off and removed the pins from her hair. She looked as beautiful as he remembered. His hands cupped her face and his lips closed the distance slowly, giving her time to stop him. But she didn't, and when their mouths touched, she melted in his hands. It was all the invitation he needed. His arms went to her back and brought her closer until their bodies touched, deepening the kiss. Her lips were so right, so soft. *Heaven.* She moaned and all his blood went to his groin. His tongue sought entrance, and when her lips opened, he explored and rammed and would have devoured her if he could. She felt supple, and giving, and responsive. Her eyes closed, her hands caressing his hair. He stooped down and grabbed her behind, lifting her. Her legs wrapped around his waist. There was need, lust and tenderness in those luscious lips, in those subtle hands. This was how it felt to have a woman who really wanted him in his arms. Even now that she knew who he was, she didn't want his power, or his money. She just wanted *him*. Compared to this, the succession of one night stands and service providers that had been his whole sexual universe before her felt wrong, superficial and pointless. He wanted *this,* and *this* didn't have a price tag.

"Get a room, you two, will ya?" the gruff voice of Hack's security chief intruded on their passion.

Hack looked at the man and grinned devilishly. "Sure, no problem." With the girl still in his arms he turned around and started his way to the bedroom.

"Let go," she said, smacking his chest one time with her fingertips. He did and she climbed down. "Mr. Wilson, are you ok?"

"I'll live, darling," he answered, smiling. His eyes lost their twinkle and became hard when they zeroed on Hack. "How the hell did I get here?" he barked.

"You know how," Hack answered levelly.

"The team?"

"Nope."

"Didn't you learn anything about security protocols in all these years?"

"It's her fault," the younger man shrugged. "She called me a cold-hearted bastard for not wanting to go help you and threatened to go herself."

"I did not call you that…"

"What kind of pussy are you that you let a woman who doesn't even have your ring on push you around?" Hubert interrupted.

Janice inhaled sharply and the older man gulped.

"Sorry, darling, this has nothing to do with you. Don't be upset," he added in a softer tone.

"Ha," Hack gloated. "Who's the pussy now?"

"This is ridiculous!" Janice waved her arms. "There are dangerous men in the building, we're trapped here, you need medical assistance, and you two are fighting about… what?"

"Procedures," the old man said. "This one here," he pointed at Hack, "is the king in this chess game. He must be protected at all costs. If he falls, it's game over."

Janice shook her head. "Whatever." She pressed her lips together and looked at each one of the men in turn, then sighed. "What do we do now?"

"*We*," Wilson stressed, "don't do anything. You two stay here while I do my job."

"Stay here? How long?" Janice's eyes widened.

"Probably the whole weekend."

"What are we going to do up here the whole weekend?" She clamped a hand on her mouth, but it was too late.

Both men smiled wolfishly.

"Get a room?" The old man winked before disappearing behind the mirror.

* * *

Yani

"Do you want to?" Hack's bass voice intruded on Yani's bewilderment.

"Want to what?"

"Get a room?" He tilted his face and grinned.

She felt her ears hot again. "My face is red, isn't it?" She spoke softly.

"Like the sweetest apple, ready to be eaten." He stepped closer but didn't try to touch her.

Yani could feel his energy surrounding her, hugging her, kissing her. She had missed him, this, so much.

She put a hand on his chest and pushed slightly. "I can't think when you're so close."

He gave her space, but not much. "Is that a bad thing?"

His fingers wrapped gently around her arms.

She took a deep breath. "We can't. There are men in the building. And now you're my boss..."

He moved one hand to her back and pushed her softly but steadily toward his chest. She could feel his heat all along the front of her body, and her girl parts started sending distractive signals.

His other hand lifted her chin gently until their eyes met. "At the cove, I thought I'd never see you again. I'm so glad you are here."

His pupils were dilated, making most of his ice blue irises disappear.

"Me too. I mean... we can't, you're my boss now," she murmured, mesmerized.

He rubbed his nose on hers. So, so lightly. "I'm the same man, you know."

Yani felt her ears go even hotter, if that was possible. She was stuck with the man of her dreams who happened to be her boss a whole weekend, with nothing to do except... get a room? The situation was overwhelming, a strange mixture of her wildest dreams and her worst nightmares.

She put her palms on his chest to push him away again, but she didn't follow through. He felt like a wall under her fingers, so solid, so protective. She stood frozen. Half of her brain was saying *stop*, the other *give in*.

He moved even closer, and she felt a lot more of his hardness. She looked down and up at his face again.

"I won't apologize for wanting you. I couldn't think of anything but having you in my bed again since you found me." His eyes bored into her soul.

"I did not…" Yani managed to feel offended.

The hand on her back pressed forward and his mouth closed on hers again silencing her pointless objections. This only increased her inner turmoil. It felt so good. This was going too fast. But it felt so good. There were men in the building!

He seemed to feel her struggle and his demeanor changed. He cut the kiss rudely and Yani felt as if the floor had disappeared under her feet.

"Are you going to play games with me? Really?"

"Games?" She was confused now.

"Do I have to put my hand down there and see for myself if you want me? Because, you know I have no issue doing it." His body radiated anger, but somehow it felt unreal, fake.

Yani didn't fall for it and shook her head disapprovingly. "That's so incredibly rude, I'm speechless," she said calmly, her eyelids half mast.

A chuckle escaped his lips while his fingers closed on her waist, bringing her to him again. "Well, I remember you liking my hands down there."

"It's not that simple." Yes, she wanted him. She couldn't deny it. He was her lover. The one that showered with her every night. The one that slept in her bed and came to her dreams. He had gotten under her skin and taken over. Yet… sleeping with the boss? They weren't at the cove anymore. This was real life and he was a public figure. Any picture with him would bring her father and Marcos to her, and to him. She couldn't let that happen. Yet, since she knew it was him, she had worked late every night hoping for his call. *Hypocrite.*

His arms engulfed her in a bear hug and his husky voice murmured in her ear, "Don't let fear take over. It's never a good adviser… I don't want you to be scared. Not of me, not of anyone. You're safe here."

He gazed into her eyes. "You're safe with me."

She sighed and rested her forehead on his chest. He cuddled her again, one hand on her back, the other on her nape, right in the place where she felt cherished. Her body trembled. She hadn't been hugged liked this in over ten years. Her need for tenderness was so deep it cut through her soul, and she hadn't even realized that before. She melted in his embrace.

"Let's go," he said softly.

"Where?" She hardly came back from daze.

"Shower. Your next and hopefully last excuse is that you have been working all day and feel dirty."

She smiled and lifted her face to look into his eyes. "How did you know?"

He took her chin, giving her a small peck on the mouth. Then he hugged her again and herded her toward the master bedroom.

"Do you think I could have managed to build a company like mine without predicting and overcoming objections?"

She looked up again and smirked, "Modesty is your middle name, hmm?"

He ignored her comment and placed another tiny peck, this time on her forehead.

"Yet, I have to admit you scared me back there for a second."

Another peck caressed her palm.

"How come?"

"You almost quit without even giving us a chance."

"That was very rude."

He grinned like a little boy. She sighed.

"Don't you dare talk to me like that again…"

"I won't."

"No. I mean it." She stopped and put hands on hips. They were already in the bedroom, and this was important. "I'm thirty years of age and done with men's bullshit. If you ever play macho-boy on me just to get what you want again, that's the last time you'll see me. I'm not an acquisition. I'm a woman! Get it?"

She braced for a fight. She wanted all the shit cleared from the path before going to bed. Because she knew that after… she would not be strong enough.

But instead of the mad bull she expected, or the cold bastard she feared, she found herself looking at sparkly eyes and a tender smile. He covered her whole body in a bear hug, and kisses rained on her cheeks and forehead and nose, before coming in full force to her mouth.

"Are you for real?" he asked, before fondling her lips with his again.

"But…" she managed to say.

"Never again. Never again. Never again," his voice came like a whispered mantra.

He sat on the bed and pulled her onto his lap. His mouth was on hers, his hands roamed her body from the waist up with free abandon. Never stopping, never pressing, as if his fingers were trying to relearn her shape.

She was completely undone. "You're a dangerous man," she murmured when he took a moment to simply hold her.

"You too, darling. And you don't even know it."

The bedroom was as dark as the rest of the house, and there was a faint woody aroma in the air. Another salt lamp tinted a corner orange, creating long shadows from the four posts bed.

"You really like salt lamps, don't you?"

He chuckled. "Not that much. Doctor's orders. It's supposed to help with my serotonin levels, or something."

"I think it's beautiful, magical."

"I'm glad you approve. Let me light some candles for you in the bathroom."

Placing her by his side, he went to another door that was on the farthest wall of the bedroom.

Yani entered the bathroom and found a kaleidoscope of light and shadow reflecting on tan marble. Hack was turning on the shower.

"Do you prefer a bubble bath?"

"No, thanks. The shower will do."

"Alright, I'll be in the office. Join me there when you're done."

Her stomach flip-flopped. This was it, there was no turning back. She nodded, and her color rose again. He trailed along her jaw with one finger and left.

Chapter 21

Hack

With the murmur of running water in the background, Hack checked the cameras. Now that Janice was safe, his analytical mind was in charge again. He couldn't believe his building was under assault. Whoever they were, whatever they wanted, they would pay for this.

He'd called Janice tonight because he just couldn't wait any longer. The episode the night before and Hubert's words had cut deep. She *was* ripe and he would be an ass if he didn't even try.

But he hadn't dreamed of spending the night with her so fast. He thought he would have to start over. No matter what Hollywood tried to sell about Hispanics, women from Catholic cultures were slow-cooker lovers. It took a lot of patience to get them into bed, but when they finally opened, they were hot like a furnace. His girl could definitely melt steel.

Luckily for him, he didn't have to wait. Unluckily for him, he had to solve this shit first.

"Chief, talk to me," he spoke into the mic.

"The backup team is out of commission."

"How come?"

"I still don't know. Just sent a buddy to see what's going on."

"What else?"

"You tell me. Where are they now?"

"One out of business in the camera room, the other two are messing around with the server."

"The client base credit card information and passwords?"

"Juicy aim. Bad luck for them, that one is just a bridge."

"But if they physically take the station, they can recover the deleted information."

"We have to stop them." Hack fingertips drummed on the mahogany desk.

"On it, cub. Stay put and let me do my job. Or even better: go make the little woman happy."

"I plan to." He hesitated a second. "Pops, be careful, or the little woman will make me go and get you again."

The man snickered. "You're such a pussy. She already has you wrapped around her little finger."

"Just be careful."

"Watch and learn, cub."

Wilson appeared in the server room from a low panel on the wall and put a silent bullet in the spine of the taller man, right under the skull. Malcolm Stewart spared only a glance at his fallen comrade before he dropped to the floor and crawled fast to the exit.

"He's getting away," Hack said.

"He will not," Wilson muttered. But that was a mistake, it gave away his position. Stewart fired his gun several times and emptied his clip in the old man's direction, catching him in the middle of the chest. The pained gasp was all the scum needed to run like the devil, make a short stop at the monitor's room, shoot his fallen partner and escape the building through a lateral door using Wilson's master key.

Hack watched in dismay as the man left, hardly controlling his burning desire to lock the building and hunt him down. *Fucking rules.*

Back in the server room Hubert moved. The old man gave a thumb up to the camera, and his other hand palmed his vest. His head fell back, and his eyes closed. Hack sighed, relieved.

As if on cue, Janice appeared. He could smell her before seeing her. It was his soap, yet on her the aroma was different, enticing. He extended his hand and she came to him. His robe clad her nude shape to her ankles. It was amazing how her presence affected his emotions. He was horny again.

He nuzzled the bare skin right between her breasts.

"Of all days, it had to be today…" Hack sighed. "I have to go and pick up Hubert again. You stay here, be my eyes."

"Is he hurt?" she asked, anxious.

"I don't think so. Those vests are the best, not even on the market yet. It hurts like the devil though."

"And the men?"

"Two down, one escaped. It's over."

She took a deep breath. Hack stood and took his little woman in his arms. *His?* He wished. The shower had worked its magic; all remnants of her resistance was gone. Problem was, the excuse to keep her around was also gone, and if he didn't close the deal before she left the building, she might run away. He hoped not, but the possibility was very real.

He kissed her softly. "Promise me something," he said.

"What?"

"That you'll stay here and be my eyes." He placed the head-set around her neck again.

"Alright," she answered gently.

* * *

Yani

Yani watched him go and the doubts came back. What was she doing? She should leave now before anything happened. The intruders were gone. There was no reason for her to stay. She shook her head. No, she had promised. Now she was bound by her word. Did he do that on purpose? Probably. She twitched her mouth to one side. This was definitely a dangerous man. One she really *really* liked.

Her eyes searched the small images sent from the cameras following his trail. He appeared in the server room, where he picked up Mr. Wilson, taking him to the elevators. When he was about to enter his office, she remembered something.

"Wait," she said.

"What?" he asked into his mic.

"The bad guys went to your office, and they took their sweet time before coming out."

"Good thinking, thanks."

Steering clear from the office, he went toward the restrooms on the tenth floor. A minute later he was entering the penthouse through the hidden door.

Yani stepped out of the office to meet him, her heart galloping.

He set Wilson on the sofa and looked at her.

"We make a good team," he said, grinning. She hinted a smile, but her eyes were glued to Hubert.

"Is he ok?"

"I'll live," the old man answered in a pained voice. "And you…" He glared at Hack.

"I know. I'm a pussy," he said, lifting his palms in surrender.

Wilson chuckled. "What did I miss?"

"We have two bodies, and one creep on the loose. Still no word from the backup team, and the thugs spent too much time in my office."

"Five bodies," Wilson corrected. Hack looked at him. "These guys take no prisoners. The door guard and the two walkers are gone too."

"Shit," Hack grunted, his eyes glossy.

Yani's eyes filled with tears. "Why would someone do something like this?"

"Fifty million dollars, maybe a hundred…" Hack answered.

"How?"

He took a deep breath. "The client database information. We have the system authorized to buy in one click, and there are ten million customers around the world. They could have raised fifty million just making them buy one cheap non-physical item from each account; an eBook or a movie. And after a security breach like that, I would be out of business."

"Well, cub," Wilson patted Hack's arm, "your spy gadgets, secret passages and crazy double security system really paid off today."

Hack nodded but seemed worried. "The creep has your key. Do we lock the shop?"

Hubert sat up, grunting with the effort, and then stood up on wobbly legs.

"I'll do it. But he won't come back this soon, and the backup team will show up eventually and take care of the locks. Meanwhile, we have work to do. First I'll check out the cameras to delete everything that shows the secret passages. Then we call in the cavalry."

"Sounds good. What do I do?"

"You. Stay. Here. If I see your ass out of the safe zone again, I will kick it to the moon. Understand?" Wilson said, shaking his finger in front of Hack's face. His boss only smiled.

The old man walked toward the mirror and disappeared through the hidden door. His stride grew stronger with every step.

When they were alone, Hack sighed.

"You're going to kill me," he said.

"Why?" She raised her eyebrows.

"Now that we're out of danger, the adrenaline is coming down fast, and the guards..." He blinked several times. "I'm sorry, darling. I can't now. Can I get a rain check?"

She sniffed, silent tears streaming down her face. "I'm not in the mood either."

He extended his hand and she took it. "Do you like to cuddle at night?"

Her mouth drew a tiny smile. "I'm a woman, of course I like to cuddle."

"C'mon. I'll give you the best cuddle of your life."

She chuckled softly and let him guide her to the bedroom.

She didn't think she would sleep at all. But as soon as she felt Hack at her back, she felt safe, and tired, and a warm darkness engulfed her.

Chapter 22

Yani

Yani woke up to a sea of sensations. Hack was kissing her shoulder and breathing in her ear. One hand was running along her waist going south, and at her back she could feel his erection. It was pitch-black. She couldn't see anything, so the sounds and tactile perceptions were enhanced.

"Can I have that rain check now?" he murmured.

Clamping one hand on her mouth, "No kisses," she mumbled.

He chuckled, "Alright, I can kiss your other lips instead." His full of promise rumbling voice did weird things to her insides. His hand squeezed gently her mound and her hips moved to meet him. "Mmm that's how I like it."

Moving a hand toward her back, between both of them, she tried to reach the tempting rod pressed against her small back.

He took her hand and moved it back to the front, not letting her reach him. "Let me pamper you," he said. "Just relax."

Her eyes closed and her body surrendered to the expert hands of her lover. The feeling of belonging she'd experienced during the day at the hut came back. It was as if time hadn't moved along, as if they'd never been apart. He turned her into her stomach and moved her hair to one side. He nuzzled her nape and rained kisses on her shoulders while the tips of his fingers caressed her back.

The kisses turned into soft bites, and he urged her to rise on hands and knees. He positioned himself at her back. She thought *this is it*, but she was wrong. Now his mouth was on her back, and his hands moved to her breasts. He nuzzled, then kissed, then licked, then bit, and his hands worked in tandem, massaging her breasts, caressing and squeezing her nipples. He worked his way down along her spine, until he arrived at her buttocks. There he bit down, and she whimpered more from surprise than pain. Her arms wobbled and he guided her upper body down, while his mouth went to her pussy.

"Oh, darling. How I've wanted to kiss you," he breathed and the vibration of his voice on her velvet sheath made her inner walls pulse. She pushed back and spread her knees more. "Thank you." He chuckled, sending small shock waves into her being.

A second later, she felt his tongue breaching her canal, while his nose played with her folds. He had turned and she was on top of his face. She thought she might feel embarrassed, but she couldn't. It felt too good. She giggled, feeling silly.

"What?" His voice was husky.

"This is…" His index finger entered her canal, "embarrassing," she moaned. "I'm …" his tongue lapped her nub, "sitting…" He sucked one lip into his mouth. She whimpered.

"Yes," he growled and the 's' sounded long, blowing hot air on her already hot flower, "right on my face," he finished and her folds felt puffy and her core heavy. He made a weird noise that resembled a horse snickering with his lips glued to her clit, which resonated along her inner thighs and curled her toes.

By now she had lost it. Her hips had a mind of their own and wiggled wildly. He took her butt with both hands to keep her in place while his tongue increased the pressure and moved fast, right on her most sensitive part.

She was wild with need. Her lower belly was pulsing. "I need you inside."

"Come for me," he answered, and his tongue increased even more its pressure and speed, while his nails dug into her cheeks.

"Ah," she said between moans, "voy a…" and she came, hard, wave after wave shaking her core, running down her legs and up to her abdomen.

He felt her release and moved at a speed she hadn't thought possible. In a second he was inside her, riding her while her passage clamped around his sex. He moved fast and deep, not letting her come down from the crest, keeping her there.

She gave in to the sensations and her body went limp, while he growled his own pleasure.

* * *

Hack

Hack looked at his sleeping beauty and sighed, a smile spreading across his face. She was so responsive, so transparent in her emotions, so easy to read and please. Dr. Quack was right: having a woman in the early morning came in handy, and variety was overrated when you had the right one at home.

He got up and pulled off the condom, tied a knot and took it to the bathroom's wastebasket. He'd never made love without it. Actually, he realized, he'd never *made love* before her. He hadn't realized before meeting this woman how many things were lacking in his life, and how many important things didn't have a price tag. Janice, pulsing around him, had no price tag.

Hack, still naked, walked silently to his office. He couldn't sleep now. Dr. Quack was not going to be happy. *So be it.* The security cameras showed that his building was buzzing with activity. His backup team was there, and the police were there. He took the headset.

"Talk to me, chief. What's going on?"

"You woke up early. How's the little darling doing?"

"She's ok, sleeping. Why do we have so many people nosing around?"

"The guards. We can't just sweep them under the rug. They're family."

"Agreed. Do you need me?"

"Not really."

"Anything I can help with?"

"Well, if you can't sleep, there is one thing you can do. Send the logs and the recordings of the secondary cameras to Renton, so they can find out what the intruders did. They partially blinded the primary set. They might have left something behind."

"I'm on it."

Chapter 23

Yani

Yani woke up for the second time, feeling luscious. The bed was cozy, the light shone softly through the windows, and her body felt deliciously tender in all the right places. Making love with Hack was even better than she remembered. He was such a generous lover. A deep, fuzzy feeling rumbled in her chest and she sighed. After that earth-shattering orgasm in the cove—her first with a man—she was his. He had ruined her for any other lover. Yet, this new encounter had sealed the deal in her heart. Now she didn't *want* anyone else. *I can't stay. I can't risk him getting hurt.* She took a deep breath and blinked away the tears. She was dangerous for him. With Marcos and her father on her trail, she was dangerous for any man. The fact that the creep was in the building didn't escape her. Maybe the client's database was not what they were after. But such a big mess for her? Could it be?

Speaking of which, where was her man? After a quick shower, she found him in the office, fully clothed and looking hot as ever.

"C'mere." Smiling broadly she obeyed, and he sat her on his lap. "Can I have my kiss now?"

Yani chuckled and kissed him. She poured her heart in that kiss, thinking it might be the last one. He hugged her tight, and she knew he understood. *Gosh, I could love this man.*

"You're working." She disentangled herself and ironed nonexistent wrinkles from his shirt with her hands. "I'll go make some coffee."

"Oh, that would be awesome. Thanks," he murmured. His eyes were glued to her chest, though. She had his bathrobe on with nothing underneath.

"How do you drink it?" she asked, standing.

"Bulletproof," he answered, but his attention was someplace else entirely.

"Hmm?"

"Never mind." He opened the robe and took her breasts in his hands, feeling their weight. His eyes lit up and she felt a jolt of electricity going right down to her belly. "I couldn't see these last night." His mouth closed on the left one. "Delicious," he murmured, while his tongue circled and enticed her peak. "I want you again," he growled, taking the robe completely off her shoulders and letting it fall.

She smiled. "I'm here."

He stood and kissed her, hugging her tightly. The kiss was deep, demanding, hungry, as if her kiss had awakened a possessive streak in him. He walked to the sofa and placed her on it with her pelvis hanging. His eyes bored into hers. Last night had been about her, but right now it was going to be about him.

She slid onto her knees. It was not his plan, but she wanted to taste him. Her hands opened his fly and took his shaft out. Even with a half erection, it was thick and purple, crossed by protruding veins. She touched the tip with her tongue, oh so slightly, and he shivered from head to toe. Their eyes met. He seemed hypnotized. One of her hands went to the base, the second to his rod. Two fingers slid carefully the foreskin down and her tongue licked the sensitive mushroom shaped head. He closed his eyes and took a shaky breath. His hands tangled in her hair, not pushing but present.

"Show me what you need," she breathed and took him into her mouth, or tried to, as he was growing fast. Her experience was very limited, but she hoped her enthusiasm would be enough. His hips moved forward carefully. Her tongue touched the tiny hole on the tip. The taste of him was fascinating; salty, musky, and hot man all over. He growled and his shaft grew even more. She took him deeper while her hands massaged him. His hands fisted her hair and he started pumping into her mouth. She kept up as best as she could, using her tongue and her hands, running her fingers under his scrotum toward the seam, and back again. She wanted to please him with all her heart, but when his rod reached full size her jaw started to hurt.

He growled again and she felt a pull on her hair. Her mouth let go, and her eyes sought his. Hack was staring at her with an intensity that melted ice. She could feel her inner folds growing wet and hot, just from his need. Her need.

"Lie down," he muttered.

She climbed to the sofa and retook the position where he had placed her before, opening her legs. It was all the invitation he needed. Hack took off his shirt and shorts in no time. Underwear, shoes and socks followed, and he just dove into her.

She was ready when he slid deep in one try, as if he owned her body. Her passage was slick by her need, and he felt perfect.

"Oh, it feels so good," she murmured.

"No condom, sweetheart," he breathed in her ear.

Her eyes widened, fear rocketing.

"Hack. No."

"Please. I don't have any here... I'm clean, and you too. Please..."

He kissed her into submission.

"I can't risk having a baby," she managed to say between kisses. He was sliding deep and all the way back out, but so slowly. And it felt so good.

"I want to feel all of you. Don't you feel the difference?"

"Oh yes!" Her mumbling became a scream when he put his hand between their bodies and pressed her magic button.

"That's how I like it."

Yani writhed beneath him, but it only increased the contact and undermined her will. It felt so right. The heat, the sweat, the way their bodies fit together, his hands holding her, the sense of belonging... He would be the perfect one to have children with, if only she were not cursed.

She sighed. "Please don't come inside."

"Relax."

She thought he was going to pump fast and furious, but she was wrong. He slid deep but slowly, and almost all the way out. He looked down at their joining, and then up to her heated face, then back to where their bodies met. His eyes had a spark of emotion that was lust, but there was so much more. She half-closed her eyelids and let go of any intruding thought. He kept pumping like this for some time, watching the show at the same time, until she wrapped her legs around him. Then he changed the way he entered her passage, bumping forcefully on her pelvis and giving her clit the attention it craved. She could feel the pressure building with each hit, and her hips took a life of their own.

Her hands went to his hair and she pulled until his mouth was on hers. Yani devoured him, mating her tongue with his. She sucked his tongue and worked it with her lips, showing him what she wanted, what she needed. He understood and pushed harder, deeper until he hit her golden spot up near her cervix. Her head went back, and she zoomed out into her own world of sensations. He chuckled, all male pride, and let his body run loose.

He came grunting, the vein of his neck visible. She peaked right after him when he started convulsing.

When Yani was recovering from her daze, she felt it. Liquid running down her thigh. Startled, she jumped up.

"Oh no. What have we done?" she blurted.

Chapter 24

Yani

"I'm sorry. I just... couldn't stop. You were not done. If I came out, you were not coming with me," Hack said. It was a lame excuse and she didn't buy it.

"Is that all you have to say?"

He sighed.

"When I saw you leaving at the cove, I felt this horrible anguish in my stomach. And now that you are here... I honestly wouldn't mind at all if this makes a baby."

"You don't understand..." Yani's voice was oh so low, just a whisper. Images of what his father or Marcos could do to him, ran across her mind at dizzying speed.

"*You* don't understand. I just said I want you to have my children," he answered forcefully, as if offended by her reaction.

She gawked at him.

"I mean it."

He picked up his clothes from the floor and walked out of the office.

Her compassion became anger.

"Don't *I* have a say in this?" She yelled at his shadow.

She shook her head in disbelief. *What on Earth?* She knew that if she was pregnant, she wouldn't have an abortion. She didn't judge others, but this was her choice. How would she raise a baby alone in her situation? He said he wanted her to have his *children...* that was plural.

Yani whipped a tear that had slid all the way to the corner of her mouth. She had been fantasizing about this man for months. He had kept her company during the terrible days in the desert. He had bathed with her and cuddled her to sleep every night. When they finally met again, it was so much better than she remembered. Yet, he was acting like an ass who thought could take decisions about *her* life without asking, and even expected her to be thankful. It was even worse, because he had no clue about what he was getting into. She was done with this shit. *Maybe if I'm not pregnant, I can become a nun.*

Well, one thing was sure. She had to leave *now.*

Yani strode to the bedroom, and found Hack getting dressed after cleaning up. She looked around. Her clothes where nowhere to be found.

"Where are my clothes?"

"Safe, until we have time to talk this over."

"We have nothing to talk about. You're crazy, and I'm leaving."

"Maybe I am, but you're not leaving."

"Are you kidnapping me?"

He sighed. "Sweetheart, please, sit here."

"Don't you dare *sweetheart* me..." she challenged, but her body obeyed him instead of her. Her legs walked to the bed and sat her beside him. "Please, give me my clothes," she tried to sound reasonable, but there was a whiny edge in her voice.

"Look. I'm fully aware I messed up real bad. I've broken all my rules, and probably yours. I'm thirty-nine, and you're the first woman who has entered my house, the first one who slept in my bed, the first one I didn't use condoms with."

Yani looked into his eyes, and the blue was sparkling with tears. Those tears called her own. She felt the same warm fuzzy feeling she had woken up with, only that deeper, so much deeper.

"That day at the cove… it was my first orgasm, and I haven't been with anyone else since then," she murmured, and her treacherous body made her lean against him.

His head snapped. His demeanor changed completely. She could feel his possessiveness.

"That's it. You stay here with me."

There was pure determination in his eyes. He was dead serious.

"This is insane. I can't live with you," she almost screamed. He didn't flinch.

"Why not? What's wrong with me?" Hack's eyes scrolled down his body, a smirk on his face. If he was trying to be funny, he was not exactly succeeding. Well, maybe it was funny, given that he was among the most eligible bachelors of this side of the world and hot as sin. But he was stepping on all her triggers at once. Not a happy picture.

She closed her eyes half-mast and took a deep breath, trying to bite her tongue and not burn any bridges… yet. "Besides trying to get me pregnant against my will and kidnapping me, there's nothing wrong with you," she quipped ironically.

A chuckle rumbled in his chest, and the tip of his fingers caressed her spine. She shook her head in reproach but showed a faint smile.

"Please give me my clothes," she pleaded.

"Your clothes are being washed. They'll be ready this afternoon. Are you staying?"

Her eyes welled, "Don't do this to me…"

"Live with me. Let's give it a shot. If it doesn't work, well, it doesn't. But at least we tried."

A single drop ran down her face. "I can't…"

"What is it? You want a ring? Have me on one knee? We can do that…"

"Of course not! Well, I mean, maybe in the future. But that's not the issue here."

He hugged her, caressing her back. "Look, I can't employ you anymore because we slept together. It's not so easy to get a white-collar job with those credentials of yours. There is a real possibility of you having my baby. That creep is on the loose... I can't send you to the streets like this. Just stay some more. A week. Let's see what happens."

The creep... Did Marcos or her father find her? The thought sent her heart on a crazy ride. She stood. She felt like a cornered wild animal.

"Wow. Stop," Hack commanded jumping up and retaining her in a bear hug.

"What's going on? Are you married? Is that what you're hiding?"

Her head snapped. "Who said I was hiding something?"

He fondled her face. "It's obvious, sweetheart. So, are you running away from your husband? Because, you know, considering how tight you were. Well..."

She sighed, melting in his embrace. "No," she whispered. Suddenly she was feeling very tired.

"Tell me the tale."

"What tale?"

"Why did you leave your country?"

Her jaw dropped. "You're not the only American who goes to Cancun, you know? Do I have an accent?"

"No. If I had to place your accent, I would say New England. Did you go to Yale?"

"Yes, I mean..." She huffed. "What makes you think I'm a foreigner?"

He chuckled.

"Besides the fake credentials? Well, second languages are an interesting thing. They place themselves as a layer over the first one. In special moments, when climaxing for example, people oftentimes revert to the native language."

She breathed in sharply. "What did I say?"

"Not much, but it was in Spanish. And, besides, your whole demeanor is of a good Catholic girl. Can't miss the inner conflict when it comes to sex."

"You, Mister," she said, poking at his chest, "are a dangerous man."

He took her hand and kissed her palm.

"You know it. Now tell me the tale. You don't look like the kind of girl that would be all alone in a foreign country with fake papers just for the fun of it."

Her eyebrows joined for a second. "And even knowing I was a foreigner, even knowing I had lied, you tried to get me pregnant? It doesn't make any sense..."

"I didn't try to get you pregnant. It was an accident..."

"Please don't insult my intelligence. I'm quite proud of it."

His mouth stretched in a half smile. "I would never dare to do that."

"Uh huh... so? What was that about?"

He sighed. "All I thought was I wanted you to be my first skin-to-skin. Since the cove, I hadn't been with anyone else either. I did try, but it felt so wrong I didn't even make it to the bedroom. And yes, I know a pregnancy changes everything and you might stay because of it, and you might hate me for having to stay."

He scratched his head. "I was not exactly planning ahead."

After three heavy breaths, he added with hurtful eyes: "Look, if you don't want my baby, we can get the morning-after pill and get it over with."

"I'm pro-life," she stated.

"Even at this stage?"

"I've never thought of it. But yes."

"Good."

She blew a raspberry.

"What?"

"How could you do something so risky? You don't even know me!"

"I know what I need to know."

"And what is that?" she challenged.

"One: you're dedicated and a hard worker. Two: you're gorgeous naked and without makeup. Three: you're transparent in your emotions and have feelings for me. Four: you're loyal and have the heart of a lion. Five: you're level-headed and have a great sense of humor. Six: you're intelligent without being self-centered. Seven: you're the best cook ever."

This last statement took her completely by surprise.

"How...?"

"Just stay. I promise to protect you, treat you well, make you come, and keep you on your toes..."

She smiled and then sniffled. "I can't..."

He sighed again, his patience growing thin. "You just said I was dangerous, and I am. I'm an expert on solving unsolvable problems. Whatever insurmountable chasm you think separates us, I can fix it."

"No. You can't." She started sobbing.

"Tell me the tale."

"I can't."

"Just tell me the tale," he insisted. "I'm going to find out anyway."

She shook her head. "I can't believe I'm telling you this..."

"Take a deep breath and go."

She breathed one time, deep and slow. Her eyes were fixed on the floor.

"My father is a small-time politician in Colombia, who has worked against the drug cartels for a long time. Three months ago, he found out the address of one of the barons' sister, and he delivered the information to the local anti-drug group, which works with the DEA.

"The group went to this woman's house and took her to a place where she suffered repeated molestation. They sent pictures to the guy's network and let him know they would release her only when he gave himself up. He did and went to jail for several lifetimes.

"Somehow this man knew my father had delivered the information, and he promised to do ten times worse to me than they had done to his sister. He broke out of prison and his whole network is after me. The last plan I heard of was to lock me up in a brothel in the jungle." She choked. "My father's solution to the problem he had caused was to pack me to Uruguay and marry me to a power grabber cocaine addict.

"I went to the cove, hiding from both of them. My friends took me as a stowaway on the romantic getaway they'd planned for months. They wanted to give me some time to recoup. But after the storm, they had to fix the boat, so I was in the open again. Coming here, even as illegal, was better than the other options.

"One of my friends contracted a guy to help me cross safely from Mexico. We walked in the desert for three days, and then hid in vans, and stayed in big groups in small houses. It was... uncomfortable, but the man delivered me in one piece to Florida. He also gave me my new identity and social security number. He advised me to use it only for low income jobs and never try to get credit with it. So... as you can see, I'm just another illegal immigrant trying to survive. I have nothing to offer but trouble."

"What's the narco's name?"

"Marcos Argüelles."

Chapter 25

Hack

The problem when you ask people to share their dark secrets is that their pain comes out also. Hack hugged Janice for what seemed like hours while she cried. He never knew a person could hold so many tears. Honestly, after a short while it got old and his compassion turned into restlessness. One of the reasons he was so successful was because he had a warrior mindset: he didn't dwell in pain and refused to be a victim, no matter the circumstances. So he did what he always did. While Janice cried, he played out different scenarios to clean up this mess. He could wipe out the guy and his cartel. He could pay him off. She could undergo plastic surgery and change her physiognomy... He would have to run the different scenarios with Hubert and Renton, analyze costs and possible success rates. Drug cartels... Couldn't she have an easier problem? Like a psycho ex-boyfriend?

"So, what's your real name?" he asked when she stopped crying.

"I need to wash my face. I must look horrible."

He kissed the top of her head but didn't let her leave. "Yeah, your face is red and bloated. And I still want you. Now... tell me your name."

She sighed. "Yanina Suarez, but my friends call me Yani."

"Oh, on the phone your friend called you Yani and not Janice. I made the leap."

"Yes. They sound similar."

"And why Simpson?"

Her lips stretched in a tiny smile. "The cartoon. The coyote said I reminded him of Lisa. I happen to agree."

He chuckled.

"I really need to go to the bathroom."

"Alright. Why don't you have another shower?"

She nodded and left, her robe forgotten. Hack couldn't help but admire the natural swing of her hips. Well, if he wanted to keep her, he'd better get busy. With forceful strides he moved to the office and put the headset on.

"Pops, talk to me."

"Glad you're around. Detective Preston is here, and he wants to ask you some questions."

"Please come upstairs first. We need to talk. Then I'll meet with the officer."

After pressing the button on top of the molding, the bars of the elevator disappeared, and Hubert was allowed to enter.

"We have a problem," Hack said.

"I know," the old man answered.

"No, another one. Janice can't talk to the police. She can't appear in the reports, and she definitely can't be exposed to the press."

"Tell me the tale," the security man demanded.

Hubert whistled when Hack finished recounting the situation, and then smirked. "Well, removing you and the girl from the story, I get to be a hero instead of the ass that had to be rescued twice. I can live with that."

Hack grinned and smacked his knees with his palms. "Alright, we're set. Bring the man up."

* * *

Preston

Jonas Preston's instructions were clear: He was supposed to take everything Mr. Hack Humphrey said at face value and that was the end of it. Mr. Humphrey's generous contributions paid for the cars, the gas and all the high-tech gadgets at the station.

Preston had been on the force for twenty years, and he was the first one to admit that life was much easier with this guy on their side. Yet the story was so ridiculous, even a rookie would pick up the breadcrumbs.

He sighed. "Alright. Let me read the report and see if it works for you.

"At 19:00 three men entered the building through the front door. They killed the doorman and went toward the surveillance room. There they waited for the walkers to finish the round. When they arrived, at 19:05, they killed them as well. The three of them were executed through clean shots on the forehead. The three bodies were hidden in a cleaning closet, where Mr. Hubert Wilson—chief of security—found them later, at 22:13. This information can be backed up by the security cameras. Of the three intruders, one was known to the victims, and has been identified as Mr. Malcolm Stewart, who worked as a security guard until yesterday."

Both men agreed. So far so good.

"At 19:10, Mr. Wilson arrived at the surveillance room to collect news from the guards. There he was disarmed and immobilized, but not harmed. They took a master key that was in Mr. Wilson's possession.

"At 19:12, two of the men left the room. Minutes later Mr. Wilson fought with the third one, injecting the contents of a syringe which was destined to him in the man's neck. Later, at 19:46, the man was killed by a clean shot to the forehead by his own partner, identified as Malcolm Stewart, before the man left the building using the key stolen from Mr. Hubert Wilson. The bullet can be identified by comparing it with the one found in Mr. Wilson's bulletproof jacket." He showed a small bag with the bullet in it.

The syringe part was a blatant lie, yet both men nodded. How on earth could Wilson take the syringe from the other man when he was at gunpoint, go all the way to the guy's back and inject him without leaving almost any signs of fight or struggle? The death could be more or less traceable as the partner was caught on camera outside the monitor room, but the syringe part was not right and, apparently, there were no cameras in the monitor room.

"Question. Who set off the fire alarm, and who canceled it?"

"They set off the fire alarm, and I canceled it," Wilson answered.

"Are there recordings to back up these affirmations?"

"No."

"If I may make a suggestion, I think the story will fly better if you set off the alarm and they cancel it."

"Are you suggesting we're lying?" Mr. Humphrey asked, and boy, the man knew how to intimidate. If Preston were fifteen years younger, it might've even worked.

"I'm not suggesting you're lying," he answered and gave them a second of relief before going forward. "I *know* you are lying."

Both men's eyes bored right to his skull.

"But," he lifted both palms, "my orders are full cooperation. And that is what I'm doing: cooperating."

"Your suggestion doesn't make sense either. If I have a situation more or less under control, I would never make a circus of it."

"What was the real reason for the alarm?"

Both men looked at each other. "I did it," Mr. Humphrey finally said. "The backup team didn't answer the phone. And this would call their attention."

"Why can't we put it in the report?"

"Because I don't want the comings and goings of my security system out in the open, nor for the firefighters to think we're playing games with them."

"So you killed the guy in the computer's room. And the second guy hit you."

"Yes."

"And who really killed the guy in the monitor's room?"

"The third thug," the chief of security said. "There is proof enough."

"Why?"

"He was out of commission with enough ketamine to sleep for a week. Apparently, they couldn't afford getting caught."

"Who really injected the guy?"

Hubert huffed.

"Is it there any risk under the circumstances to have an innocent man murdered in that thug?"

"No," Preston conceded.

"I did it, then," Wilson pressed.

"Alright, I give up." He scribbled a note about the fire alarm and passed the paper to Wilson. "Please, read carefully the full report, and sign. You too, Mr. Humphrey."

Wilson walked Preston out of the building. "Son," he said, putting a hand on the younger man's shoulder. "I just want you to know that we're the good guys, ok?"

Preston raked his hair with his fingers. "I know," he answered. "It's just…"

"I know," the other man interrupted, nodding. He patted his shoulder one more time, turned around and walked back into the building.

Preston shook his head. They were hiding someone. Who would that be?

Chapter 26

Hack

"How's damage control going?" Hubert asked from the door of Hack's office. Renton, the head of his personal security team, which doubled as the backup team, was beside him. The soldier looked worried, and with plenty of reason.

"So far so good." Hack's eyes didn't lift from the screen. He had spent a good deal of the morning giving Skype interviews to different media and publishing press releases, saving the company's image. Everyone wanted to know if the client's database had been hacked. He was proud to be able to say the information had been kept safe at all times. He made a note to give a bonus to his press team. Their pristine organization had saved his ass, and they hadn't even needed to come to the office.

"So, Mr. Renton, let me hear it," he commanded the other man.

"I have no accurate information yet, sir. But my guess is poison in the food."

"Symptoms?" he asked.

"We were knocked out, sir. The whole group slept over fourteen hours, and we probably could have kept going."

"What did you eat for dinner?"

"Chinese."

"How could they possibly know you were going to order Chinese?"

"That's not hard, sir. We eat it every night."

"They did their homework," Hubert mused.

"No doubt," Hack answered.

Behind the men, Janice had entered the room and was making motions with her hand, trying to catch Hack's attention. She had his cycling gear on, probably the only item in his wardrobe that almost fit her. The shirt was extremely large, but she seemed to fill in the pants quite well.

For a second, he felt outraged by the interruption, but then he remembered who was interrupting. He would probably have to get used to this if he wanted to keep her. Besides, she had been waiting with no clothes in his room for hours. Would he be so patient? Probably not. Above all, it was hard to keep a straight face with her looking so cute.

His men sensed her presence and turned.

"Well, hello there, darling," Wilson said, smiling. "Did you sleep well last night?"

"Hi, Mr. Wilson." She smiled while her face turned red. "Yes, very well. Thank you."

"What is it?" Hack interjected.

"Sorry to interrupt, but I have to go out for a little while now. I just wanted to let you know so you don't…" she looked at Renton and didn't finish.

"That's not a good idea."

She gave him a killing glare and put hands on hips. "Well, I'm hungry. And I need to cook for the whole week. I have to go buy groceries, and at least get my pots and pans. And I need clothes, and my plants have to be watered…"

"It's not safe to go out there at this time. We'll figure out how to solve this issue later. But now I'm busy," Hack dismissed her. He didn't know why, but the thought of her out of the building fisted his gut.

"I was just letting you know. *I don't need your permission,*" Janice said the last words carefully and slowly as if talking with a little child, while her eyes darted fire.

Hack was fast becoming enraged. He was not used to people challenging his authority.

"Oh no, cub. Here I put my foot down," Wilson interrupted, sounding nonchalant. "My joints need this girl's cooking, and someone's gonads do too."

Hack scowled at his chief of security, then froze. There was a warning in Hubert eyes that gave him pause. The man had been married thirty years. He probably knew how to choose his battles when it came to women. "Alright, Pops, you go with her. If she doesn't come back for any reason, don't bother to come back at all."

Janice's eyes grew larger in surprise.

"If you don't come back, you are responsible for him becoming homeless, understood?"

"You're using my affection for him to manipulate me…"

"Yes, I am." He smirked. "C'mere."

"What?" she said, giving him a hard look, but walking forward anyway.

He took a wristwatch from a drawer and put it on her. "See the time? It's 11:00 am. I want you back by two o'clock sharp, or I go get you."

"You're impossible!"

"You know it."

She growled and stormed out.

"Take care of my girl, alright?" Hack told the old man, his eyebrows pulled together.

"I will. I have a vested interest, remember?" He winked and strode after her.

Renton watched them go with one side of his mouth quirked. He surely recognized her from the cove. For some reason, Hack found the hinted smirk insulting. That girl, with her ridiculous clothes and the cocky attitude, had done more last night for his business than the six goons this man commanded.

"Well, Mr. Renton. I'm not happy with your performance, *at all*. I pay you very good money to sit every night with your buddies and play cards, so once in a while you can be available to me. The one time I happened to need you, you were not available."

"I know, sir. It's unacceptable," the man answered. Set up or not, they had opened the door to their demise by having an openly predictable behavior, and he knew it.

"How are you going to compensate me? And what steps are you going to implement so it doesn't happen again?"

"About the availability issue, I'm thinking about moving the center of operation to your rooftop, if it works for you. I just noticed you have a one-bedroom apartment with kitchen and bathroom by the pool.. And I guess buying food as a group will be out of the question from now on. Regarding compensation, state your price. As always, whenever or whatever the task, my team will respond."

"Fair enough," Hack answered. "Any comment about our visitors' whereabouts?"

"Yes, they spent several minutes testing the security bars of your elevator and looking for hidden switches. Then they went to the main server room and pulled out the files containing the building's electricity circuits."

Hack's eyebrows jumped. "Not the client database?"

"No, sir. And this is why I want to move our base closer. Their movements indicate they were after you personally, not the data."

Hack felt a lump in his throat. "What if they weren't after me? Bring the helicopter to the roof. Wait for instructions."

"Yes, sir."

* * *

Yani

Yani fumbled with the lock, mumbling incoherent curses in Spanish.

"You shouldn't be speaking in that language, you know," Wilson said to her, his voice patronizing.

She blew a raspberry. "What's the point? I know you know."

"Just don't do it," the old man said, "and, please, give me the keys."

Yani put her apartment's keys in the old man's and and saw in dismay how he locked the door from the inside and leaned his back on it, tucking her keys in his pocket.

"Go get your stuff, and let's get out of here. I have a bad feeling."

She looked at him with contempt. "Doesn't it bother you, what he said?"

"Darling, no offense… but if I can't protect you or you outsmart me, then I am useless for my job and retirement is in order."

"And the homeless part?"

The old man smirked. "That's because I live in the building, so I would be literally homeless. A homeless man with a fat bank account. Enough to buy a house by the beach and live comfortably bored for the rest of my life."

The girl looked at him and her eyes welled. "He's a good man," she said.

"Don't go getting ideas of protecting him against his will. He won't take it." Wilson sighed. "Please, just get your stuff, ok?"

"What did Hack say when he called?" Yani asked while putting some clothes inside a bag. Her studio was tiny, but well designed. It had completely open floor plan, and her drawers were in the base of her bed.

"They weren't after the money. They were trying to reach the penthouse. He wanted us to turn around and go back. He even had the helicopter ready to pick us up in the middle of the street if necessary."

Yani snorted.

"So… as you can imagine, we're cutting the shopping short. Hurry up and let's get out of here before he does something foolish."

She nodded and went toward her patio. Her plants needed tending.

"Wait," he said. "What's out there?"

"A balcony."

He drew his gun, "Stay here."

Wilson pushed the sliding door slowly, looking to one side and then the other. While he was opening the mosquito mesh door, a knife sank into his right shoulder. He gasped and the gun fell from his hand.

Everything seemed surreal. He was falling to the floor, ripping the mesh as he went. There was blood everywhere. Yani's first impulse was to run toward Hubert to help him. Until she saw the creep coming after her. It was the same one who had assaulted her, the same one who had broken into the building. She ran toward the door, but it was closed, and Wilson had her keys. The man was already entering the living room, jumping over the old man's bleeding body.

She hurried to the kitchen looking for anything she could use. When the man came in, she had her pan ready.

She swung it with all her might.

The man turned and it hit him on the back. He kept spinning, locking onto the pan with his arm, and the handle flew from Janice's hands, hurting her fingers.

She ran toward the stove and threw a pot at his head. It hit him, and the man cursed.

Yani opened the drawer, took her kitchen shears and sprinted.

"Oh no, bitch." He caught her flying hair and pulled her to him.

She aimed at his face with the scissors, but the man was faster. He blocked her with his forearm, and the blades sank in. He growled in pain but didn't release her.

She squirmed, and he backhanded her.

Yani lost her footing. His fist, closed tight in her hair, stopped her fall.

"You are coming with me," he said through gritted teeth with the blade still stuck in his arm.

He slapped a foul-smelling handkerchief over her mouth and nose.

Everything went black.

Chapter 27

Hack

Hack's cell phone rang with a tone he'd wished never to hear. His hand snaked and picked up. "Speak to me."

"He's got her." Hubert's voice came out strangled. "Hurry..."

Hack cut the call and rang Renton.

"Yes?" The man's voice was alert.

"Wilson's down at Janice's apartment. Send two men there with a paramedic kit, and join me at my place. Be ready to hunt."

Hack's fingers flew across the keyboard. William Theodore Humphrey was called *Hack* for a reason. By the age of twelve, he had hacked the CIA servers for the first time, by twenty, there was no place he couldn't enter. He was left alone, mostly because he didn't use the information; he came from old lineage and his father knew how to deal with power. When he founded II. H. LLC. and set his mind on building an online empire, most of the secret service agencies of the world sighed in relief.

He gained access to the satellite just over their heads at that moment and located Janice's wristwatch signal.

"There you are." He placed Google maps information on top of it. His eyebrows shot together, a deep crease cutting his forehead. "Where are you taking her?" The direction was clear, too clear for comfort. "No, no, no... not the airport."

The alarm distracted him. Renton was coming.

"Is the helicopter ready?" he asked the moment he felt the other man's presence.

"Yes."

"Let's go. We need to catch a plane,"

"Understood." Renton took his phone out. "Get the helicopter and team ready to leave."

Hack picked up his laptop and satellital phone and strode to the door with the other man in tow. Taking the stairs two by two, they climbed to the rooftop, where the door opened by fingerprint and code.

He could see the men jumping into the helicopter, and the pilot turning the rotor on, while he ran low to reduce the exposure to the blades' wind, and climbed the chopper, with Renton right behind him.

"Teterboro," he yelled over the noise. The pilot gave him the thumbs up, and the bird flew.

* * *

Malcolm Stewart

Malcolm Stewart patted the limp body of the girl, looking for a cell phone or anything she could use to communicate. There was nothing.

The wristwatch was interesting though; a man's watch, expensive and too bulky for her slender arm. He unhooked it and put it on his own wrist. She wouldn't need to know the time where she was going. He smirked and lifted her t-shirt to look at her medium-sized breasts. That was a fine-looking woman.

"Snap out of it." His own voice broke the silence of the parked van. The orders had been crystal clear: not a finger on her, or the boss would personally cut off his dick and shove it up his ass.

He opened a wooden box and placed the girl inside, making sure the cushions were in place and she had air to breathe. His arm hurt like the devil, but he ignored it. The unpolished surface read *fragile* on the four sides, and had a red arrow pointing up. The box slid easily over the side platform down to the dolly load, and he carried his trophy toward the private jet, whistling.

A short, bulky man with dark glasses and an impeccable suit peeked inside the box and nodded once. Another man, dressed the same, came down the stairs with two sports bags and placed them in Malcolm's hands.

Malcolm took them and walked nonchalantly back to his van. There was no need to count the two million dollars. From his time as a courier, he knew a million weighed twenty-two pounds, just about what he was carrying now in each hand. Neither did he need to check inside. For good or for bad, Marcos's word was always gold.

What now?

The van cruised easily through the airport exit and headed north toward Norwalk. Connecticut was a charming place with plenty of money. It would be easy to find a cozy house in a neighborhood surrounded by woods where a new millionaire would not draw much attention. He could say he was an online retailer, just like Hack Humphrey. The key in his pocket was tempting. Maybe he could pay them another visit, this time for the database, and get a house by the ocean instead, and a boat. He'd always wanted a boat. Nah, the key was as good as a piece of metal by now, and he had no chance to enter that building without getting a bullet in his forehead. Better just be a millionaire.

When he left the highway and took the coastal road, he was feeling quite proud of himself. That was until he saw the chopper hovering in midair and two men with automatic weapons pointing at him.

He stepped on the breaks and did a U-turn.

The van fell on its side with a powerful jolt. Quick bursts of gunfire had blown out the two tires on which the careening vehicle rested.

Shaking off the hard impact, he unhooked the safety belt and looked at the money, but he didn't try to reach for it. There would be another job, maybe.

He pulled his gun and checked the safety, opened the passenger's seat door with a push and jumped out while squeezing the trigger.

He didn't make it far. The helicopter came after him as he sprinted and he was knocked to the ground, a two hundred fifty pound gorilla on his back, and the cyclops's eye of a gun barrel pressed to his skull.

He tried to breathe, and managed to get some air into his lungs, let go of his weapon and put hands in front of him.

"Alright, you've got me. Get off," he managed to say, but the other man didn't flinch.

"She's not here," a voice yelled.

The weight came off his body, and he was pulled up by the collar of his jacket. A very angry Hack Humphrey loomed before his eyes, as did a powerful fist ready to hit.

"Where is she?"

"Colombia." He gulped.

* * *

Hack

Hack looked at the ceiling of his helicopter, took a deep breath and made up his mind. His fingers dialed a number he'd sworn never to dial again.

"Well. What a pleasant surprise."

"Hello, Father." He played cool. None of them bought it.

"So, what can I help you with?" No gloating? What was wrong with the man?

"I'm about to go into full blown hacking mode. Tell your partners I'm just looking for a friend and their secrets are not threatened."

"Wait!"

"What?"

"You don't want to do that. People are not in the right mindset at this time. I won't be able to bail you out."

"I have no choice."

"Let me help you."

"Why?"

"You're my son, for fuck's sake!"

Hack didn't answer. His controlled but heavy breathing was his response.

The man in the phone sighed. "Give me a second."

"…" Silence was Hack's only response.

"Alright. I'm sending you login information for the Mossad database. Your sat phone. Encrypted. It's a complimentary one-day account. You should be able to find her if your friend is anywhere on the surface."

"How did you know it was a *she*?"

"Only for a woman you would go into full shining-armor mode. I'm glad you found one worth fighting for."

"I have to go." Hack cut the conversation. His father sounded really strange. Helped him without asking anything in return?

Hack decided to leave that line of thought for later and hacked into Teterboro database.

"Renton."

"Yes, sir," his main man answered.

"Is the pilot ready?" Hack asked.

"Yes, sir."

"We need a flight plan to Colombia, as fast as possible, and get ready to leave in under one hour."

"Where exactly in Colombia, sir?"

"Use Bogota. I still don't know." Hack bit back his frustration.

"Any idea of the terrain?"

"Probably deep jungle, hopefully rivers. Could be mountains. Take the boat, light ammunition, climbing gear and a machine gun for noise."

"On it," the seasoned soldier answered and typed orders in his phone.

Hack realized at that moment he could be leading his men to death.

Was he ready to die? *No.*

He gritted his teeth.

They were bringing his girl back.

No casualties.

Period.

God, if you are up there… this would be a good moment to show your hand and help me out. I'll pay you back.

Chapter 28

Yani

Yani woke up on a comfortable bed. Her head hurt like the devil, though, and her mouth felt pasty. She didn't move but tried to feel her surroundings. There were insects and birds' sounds, and the temperature was warm. A soft breeze brought the aroma of soaked dirt and plants. She was *home*.

The bed bent under the weight of another person sitting down.

"Yani," a familiar voice spoke softly. "C'mon, get up. You need to drink some water."

Two fingers touched her forehead softly.

"Go away." She pushed the hand, turned and curled up into a ball.

"C'mon, baby, don't be mean…"

Her eyes snapped open and she turned around to face at the owner of the voice. "Me? Mean? You kidnap me and I am the one who's mean?"

He smirked. "Glad you chose to wake up. Now drink…" he said, bringing a glass to her lips.

"Don't touch me." She moved away from him until her back was on the headboard of the bed, and lifted her knees, protectively.

"Alright. Here. Drink." He extended the glass to her.

She accepted the water and gulped. She hadn't realized how thirsty she was.

"Slowly, or you won't keep it down."

"Marcos, where am I?" she asked, giving back the glass, and looking at her former sweetheart's face. He was the same as he'd been when they were teenagers, yet a completely different man. His eyes were hard and haunted, and a deep line bisected the middle point between his eyebrows, even when his face was relaxed.

"You're in one of the plantation houses in the jungle."

A tear fell down Yani's face. "You know I'm very sorry about what happened to Silvia, don't you?"

His jaw locked. "I know. Your father is *un hijo de puta*, though."

"He said he wouldn't have done it if he'd known…"

"It wasn't her. It was a pro. The whole thing was staged. He planned everything to the last detail to set me up."

"So Silvia is ok?" Hope for her childhood's friend shone in Yani's eyes.

Macos shook his head. "She is traumatized but could be a lot worse. She was forced to watch, was told every time she was next. She was roughed too. They used her panicked face for close ups."

"But he wouldn't…"

"Oh yes, he would."

She sighed.

"C'mon, Yani. He hates me and you know it."

"Yes. I know."

He smirked. "Good. Smile."

"What?"

Before even finishing the word, Marcos had taken a picture of her with his phone and sent it.

"What just happened?"

"I just let your dad know you are home."

He smirked again.

Yani gawked.

Reality came back, crushing down on her shoulders. She was just a peon in a hate game. She knew it, but for a second, talking about

Silvia, she felt they had gone back to the time when they were the best friends in the whole world. She was wrong.

"I'm not at home."

"Yes, you are. We are finally together, and this is our home."

"You don't get it, do you? We are done since you cheated on me."

"That's the way of the *soldado.*"

"Well, you were not a *soldado* when we started dating. I never wanted you to be one."

He shook his hands, exasperated. "And what was I supposed to do to give you the life you were used to? Be a corrupt politician like your father?"

"My father is not corrupt!"

"Yes, he is. No honest politician ever makes it into office, and you know it. The only reason he started fighting the cartels was because of us. And he doesn't fight the others. Just me."

She gaped at him.

"I'm much better than your father, you know? He's a paper doll made of false promises and manicured hands, just a front man. I give back to the people. I take care of them and their families. I feed them, dress them, put a roof over their heads and give them a sense of belonging. All your father and his kind do is to steal our dignity and treat us like slaves."

Janice huffed. "And what do I have to do with that?"

"Nothing."

"Then why am I here?"

"You are my girl."

"Not anymore."

"Yes, you are. I made sure of that." He sneered. "Why do you think a beautiful woman like you was almost never asked out on a date, and when you were, the guys never showed up?"

"You?"

"Yes. I knew you were upset and needed some time to accept what I had to offer. But I never gave up on you. I made sure I was your only one."

Hack's face growling his release crossed Yani's mind. Marcos was not her only one, not anymore. He was not the man she thought about when she was alone either. He was just a mistake of her past; a huge mistake, considering the present situation.

She was thinking fast, though. What would the man he'd become do if he found out? Just in case, she decided to steer the conversation in a different direction. "And why now?"

"Because you're ripe." He touched her face tenderly and she smacked his hand away. He smirked again. What had happened to the boy she had fallen for? He used to have such a beautiful smile.

"You said you were going to lock me up in a brothel," she accused him.

"That's where we are right now. Safest place in the world." His arms opened, taking in the place.

"But you made it sound like…"

"Like I was going to share you? I know. That was for your father. Let him wonder."

She sighed. "How did you find me?"

"I never lost you. Well, except for those days in Marita's boat. You scared me there."

Her brows furrowed. "What do you mean?"

"The time you spent in Cancun was the only time I lost track of you. Other than that, I was there every single minute."

"In the US too?"

"Manuel is one of my people. Do you really think just any illegal immigrant going North can get a fake identity and a social security number? No, my dear. That is only for us, business partners with immunity."

Her eyes grew large in surprise.

"You wouldn't have survived that life. That's why I helped you."

She didn't say anything, so he went on.

"The gringos only want us for slave work, just like the politicians here. Illegal women can only work as maid, babysitter or whore. Anything else is off limits. I sent you to Fabiane's so you had a taste of a real illegal immigrant's life in a safe environment, but I was sure you would do something with the ID. I was right. New York. Wow. You think big. I'm proud of you."

She rested her forehead on her arm, refusing to give in to his praise. Any hint of trust had been taken away with that picture, and to think he'd been manhandling her entire life from the shadows was nightmarish.

He scooted closer and combed her hair with his fingers.

"I had a life, and you destroyed it," she said, sobbing. She wasn't really sure at this point if she'd ever had a life. Except for the days with Hack, everything had been orchestrated. Well, if she had to make an assessment those days had been the best, somehow that simple fact made her feel a lot better about herself.

"Yes, the bank. Accounting degree in Bogotá, MBA from Yale. Youngest president ever in any of the branches. I'm very proud of you, you know? You can have it again, with me. I want to open a bank. I want to loan money to people to buy houses and fields. You can do that."

"You want to use me to launder drug money? Are you crazy? It's dirty money." He couldn't be serious, could he? He was expecting to use her knowledge for his purposes? Had he orchestrated her choice of career as well? How?

"All money is dirty, sweetheart. The concept of money itself is dirty."

"I don't agree with you."

"I don't care." He kissed the top of her head and got up from the bed. "The bathroom is over there, and there's a dress on the chair. Get yourself pretty. We're going to have dinner and go to bed early. We have a lot to catch up on."

* * *

"We don't have permission to land in Colombia, sir, only in Brazil," the pilot's voice came out of the speakers.

Hack's head snapped up from his computer and looked at the intruding box. "What happened?"

"They didn't say. They just changed their mind," the voice answered.

"How about the fuel?"

"Enough to get to Brazil if we steer now."

"Suggestions?" Hack asked Renton, who was listening alert. His men were also waiting for instructions.

The man shrugged. "We can always jump."

"And how do we get out of there? We need to get to Brazil."

"Let me see the map."

Hack placed the laptop on the other man's lap.

Renton studied it carefully, running his finger over rivers and mountains, then zoomed in the satellite in certain areas until he could see people and vehicles.

"I think our best way out is water. Here," he pointed at the map. "The plantation where they have her is very close to the Vaupés River. This is probably how they take the produce out. If we follow the river, we can make it to Yauareté across the border, and then we're on safe ground. The airport of Iauarete is three kilometers east from the village."

"Alright, let's do it." Hack's jaw set with determination.

Chapter 29

Yani

Reluctantly, Yani took a shower and put the dress on. It was a yellow sundress with spaghetti straps that hugged her torso to her waist and then fell loose to mid-thigh. She hadn't worn a dress like that in ages, not since she'd left Marcos actually. At the beginning she was depressed and didn't want any man close. Later on, she wanted to look professional. And after moving to the US, well, she was just afraid even to be seen.

Yani knew that the clothes had a meaning. If she wore them, she was accepting Marcos's terms. She didn't want to, but what was she supposed to do? Put Hack's clothes on again? They were dirty and reeked of urine. How long had she been knocked out? She opted for using the dress and the low sandals but avoided the makeup bag that sat on the chair. She hoped it was enough to make a statement. She doubted he cared though. There was no underwear, and she had to go commando. She didn't like it one bit.

A key turned in the door, and Marcos appeared. With a black open shirt and white pants, he looked dark and dangerous and handsome as ever. They said he had royal Inca blood, and she didn't doubt it. He was originally from Peru, after all... But she had to remember and keep remembering he was also a cold-hearted bastard who had transformed her entire life in a mouse maze, one who killed and destroyed without regret. She remembered Mr. Wilson. Poor man, how he had loved her soup.

"You look beautiful," he said huskily.

"I'm not using the dress for you. I just had nothing else to wear," she told him, and crossed her arms in front of her body, pouting. *What's wrong with me? I'm acting like a teenager all over again.*

His smile grew to a grin. "I know. But by the end of the night, you'll take it off for me. That's all that counts."

"I won't."

"Yes, you will." There was a dark shadow in his eyes. "After you." He opened the door and let her pass.

Yani found herself in another room. It seemed like a living/dining area. The table was set for two. It was an odd room. Besides the table, there were two dancing poles framing a big flat screen television and an entertainment center with huge speakers. In front of the TV, a massage black leather recliner was the only sofa available.

Marcos pulled a chair out and nodded at her. She sat, and he uncovered the food: grilled payara on banana leaves, and, as a side, fried plantain and maize with vegetables. Yani laughed when she saw the food, she couldn't help it.

"You remember?" Marcos asked anxiously, and she saw a hint of the boy she had fallen in love with so long ago.

"How could I not?"

The payara was a classic of the many rivers of Colombia, just like the piranha. It was a scary-looking thing with huge inferior canines—to the point that one of its names was vampire fish. One day, they were fishing, and she had caught a payara too big for her. The wrestling match with the fish made her lose her footing. Marcos caught her right as she was about to dive into the river headfirst and, possibly become lunch herself. That day they kissed for the first time and their relationship changed forever.

He brought two champagne flutes and gave her one. All of the sudden, Yani was having a hard time staying upset with him. But she had to. Anger was her only defense in a situation where she was otherwise helpless. They ate in silence. The fish was on the salty side, and she finished her glass in no time, much faster than she was used to. The effect hit immediately.

"Marcos, I'm not feeling well."

"What do you feel, darling?" he asked with his full attention on her.

"I feel... bubbly." She giggled. She wasn't a drinker and had gone without food for more than a day. The wine was hitting her hard and fast. *I have to fight it.* She giggled again.

"It's the sparkling wine. Some water will help." He got up and brought a glass to her. "Drink," he said.

"Thank you," she downed the water. It tasted weird, but she was not in condition to complain.

Yani played with her food, feeling uneasy. Marcos seemed fixated on her face, as if waiting. Something was not right.

She felt increasingly hot. It was like the heat of being caught in Bogota's traffic without air conditioning added to the nights they spent together when they were teens. It felt as if his need for sex was all around her. A single drop came running down her forehead. She was sweating.

Marcos got up and went to the entertainment center, pushing some buttons. Electronic music came out of the speakers, and lights pulsed with many colors. The room looked like a nightclub. The lights were so... weird. They seemed to morph, as if they were alive. The bass speaker hit her bones, giving her goosebumps. Not just a light whisper crawling along her spine. It was her whole back, and it didn't go away. Soon the caress of her skirt over her legs felt like pure sensuality. And she wanted to dance more than anything, with the exception of making love. She wanted to make love even more than to dance. Why was it so hot in here?

"I need more water," she said.

"Let's dance." Marcos took her hand and led her toward the empty space in front of the TV.

He started to slow dance even though the music was anything but slow. Every touch felt like liquid lust. Her senses were deeply enhanced. Her body started a sinuous contortion she couldn't—or didn't want—to stop. The lights seemed to beam, and merge and morph. It was as if she were immersed in a crazy giant kaleidoscope that pushed her in several directions at the same time.

"Marcos, I'm thirsty," she pleaded. *Maybe water will make the heat go away.*

"I'll give you some later," he murmured in his ear.

Yani was melting inside. If Marcos didn't take her right here, right now, she would die of need. Something was definitely wrong.

"Marcos," she murmured, "what did you put in the water?"

"I told you you would take that dress off for me tonight…" His hand pushed her to him and she could feel all of him against her. He was ready, just waiting for her resistance to melt away.

He took her hand and pressed it on his shaft over his pants. "Want this? You are going to have to work for it. You're going to dance the pole for me, while you take your clothes off." He nosed her neck and set it on fire. "You're going to do all sorts of things for me…" His finger trailed up her back, and she started to lean on him more. "You're going to do everything I tell you to…" The back of his hand brushed over her nipple and she groaned, unable to stop herself. "You'll see. You're going to love being my favorite doll." His mouth opened on her neck and sucked hard. She felt she would die of pleasure.

What's wrong with me?

Yani remembered the foul taste in the water again and it hit her. *He drugged me.* She'd read about these funny looking pills in the news… they had caused many deaths at an electronic party in Buenos Aires. *This is not real. I have to fight it,* one side of her mind murmured. *What for? I'm stuck here at his mercy. Hack will never find me.* Hack's name did it. She could be carrying his baby. She had something to cling to now as she struggled to regain her consciousness. *Hack.* It was true, he might never find her. But she knew he would try. She had to resist. Go down fighting.

"I can't," she said, pressing her legs together. "Please, I need water."

"Oh, you are getting higher now," he studied her face with knowing eyes. "You're feeling it all the way to your core. You want me to take you, don't you? I wanted to take you slow, make you dance for me… but what the hell, let's go to the bedroom."

He walked while dancing. Yani fought her own skin, her own needs, her resistance fluctuating wildly.

Once they were away from the lights, part of her ability to think came back. The music was still strong, but at least it didn't surround her.

He pulled the straps down and cupped her breasts.

"I can't. I love someone else." She struggled, trying to keep Hack's face on her mind.

"It doesn't matter who you daydream about, darling. I'm your only man, always have been, always will be." He pulled her toward him and kissed her, his hands trailing down and getting a hold of her buttocks.

She pushed him hard and sat on the bed.

His eyes rounded.

"I slept with someone else, and I loved it," she blurted. She had never felt like this in her whole life. She felt she would die if she didn't have a man, any man, between her legs. But she fought it, knowing it was not real, and that if she held strong long enough it would pass.

"You're lying," he growled.

A vibrator could get her out of this mess. *My kingdom for a rabbit.* She squeezed her eyes. "Didn't you see the clothes I was wearing? They were man's clothes, and too big for me. They were my lover's."

Marcos strode to the bathroom and came back holding her clothes.

"You, whore!" he snarled and backhanded her. She welcomed the pain; it helped her fight the other emotions. She suspected it would've hurt a lot more if she weren't drugged.

"Yves Saint Laurent? You got yourself a loser who likes to pretend he's rich?" He picked her up by the hair, "Who is he?" he fumed, nose to nose. "Tell me the name of the bastard I have to kill."

The impulse was too strong, and he was too close. She kissed him. He pushed her away and wiped his mouth with the back of his hand. "You. Dirty. Bitch. Who is he?"

That did it. All the heat transformed into a big ball of pure hate. She stood and faced him, hands on hips and rage in her eyes.

"I'm dirty? I'm a bitch? You're such a sore loser! You thought you could keep me on a leash? Well. You lost! I cut the leash and got myself a man. One that actually made me cum. Not like you. You think you took my virginity? Think again. You just broke my hymen. My pleasure belongs to another." She spat venom with each word, ten years of hurt and anger taking hold and coming out. "How does it feel to know you're not the only one? It hurts? Good! It's not even close to how I felt when I saw you with that other girl. Like a knife ripping my heart, like what I had given you was worth nothing to you, like my love and devotion meant nothing to you. I felt stupid, and defiled. Waiting with my clothes in a bag, ready to run away with you, leave my life behind for you… and you sleeping around!" She realized she was about to cry. She couldn't allow it. Not now. She had to keep fighting. *Hack. He wants to kill Hack.* She needed to change the target of his rage. And she knew exactly how to do it.

Yani forced herself to laugh without humor. "All these years scaring away guys and it was you who actually pushed me into his arms. I'm glad I was with another man, I'm glad I found out how it felt to be fucked right so I realized what a lousy lover you really are. No wonder you need to drug women to sleep with you. *Nobody would want you otherwise.*"

He stood tall and looked at her, his eyes murderous. "I was going to make you my favorite doll, build a bank for you, be the one to have my children. But now that you like being a whore, I'll let you have your wish. You'll go to the front of the house and be fucked twenty times a day. You'll be high all the time and lovin' it, and your videos will be all over the web for your fucker and your father to see."

He grabbed her by the arm and pushed her out of the second room to a long hallway. She was too dizzy to walk or fight, so he dragged her.

When they had made just a couple of feet from the door, a man came running.

"Comandante, the fields are burning!"

He dropped Yani and sprinted toward the far end of the corridor.

* * *

Marcos

"Talk to me," Marcos demanded while putting the bulletproof vest on and grabbing a sawed-off shotgun.

"We don't know who they are. One of the farmers saw five jumpers, military style, gringo looking. They set the west fields on fire and ran into the jungle."

"DEA?"

"Don't think so. They look like mercenaries."

"Send everyone after them. I want them alive enough to give me information."

"All of them? What about the house?"

"I said all of them. I. Want. Those. Men!"

Marcos pulled his phone and called his main adversary and former boss, Alberto Ramos.

"What a surprise," a silky voice answered.

"Did you send the goons? Are we at war?"

The other man inhaled sharply. "Not that I know of. Are you under attack?"

"Gringo goons just set my jungle on fire. If it's you, I want to know."

"It's not me, Marcos. I give you my word."

"I believe you. Have to go."

"Keep me informed, and if you need help, just ask."

"Thanks, bye."

Marcos walked toward the main hall. His men were getting ready to hunt. He also saw the big screen that showed the video feed from the front rooms, each one with a woman inside. Some of them were in fetal position, crying. He felt a pang of anguish. Would he really put his Yani there? He looked out the window and his heart turned into a fist. The girl he had fallen in love with was no more. This woman was a witch with a sharp tongue. Whether it was true or not that she'd managed to get a lover, she had chosen her words to hurt his male pride. And she had succeeded.

Now she's going to pay a hefty price for her victory.

Chapter 30

Hack

Two men had stayed behind with Hubert, so the team was reduced to six: four soldiers, Renton and Hack. Finding the plantation was not hard once Hack accessed the Mossad database. Everything was there, under the Marcos Argüelles file: properties, movements, bank accounts, army details, and even his personal life. This is how Hack found out the man had dated Janice. His mouth twisted in a rueful half-smile when he saw this. Hadn't he wondered why the problem couldn't be easier, like a psycho ex-boyfriend? Life had a wicked sense of humor sometimes. One thing that bugged him was that Janice hadn't mentioned her relationship with the guy. Would have he acted the same way if the roles were inverted? *Probably.*

They went for it, no time for finesse. One man stayed in the plane, in case there was trouble at landing. The other five jumped and torched the fields. The three soldiers ran into the jungle, making enough noise to be easily followed. They would then come back to the river and get the boat ready. Hack and Renton were going in. Renton was not happy about it, but Hack was not in the mood to play king in the chess game. *What's a king's life without his queen? Just purposeless and tedious responsibility.*

It was a weak plan. The boat falling from a plane could be intercepted, even when Hack's toys made sure it landed on the best possible location. Being their only transportation out, a mistake could leave the team stuck in the jungle.

Hack and Renton ran to the main house in a low crouch and stayed flat on the floor behind some bushes, waiting. They watched when a group of about twenty men left, armed to the teeth. It was not going to be easy for Renton's guys to shake them. They heard an automatic weapon spitting and about five men fell into the dirt. They didn't move again. The others hit the ground two seconds later, but moved ahead fast, snaking like cobras in the sun.

Renton glanced at Hack and grinned. It looked like one of the guys had deviated from the initial plan, but it had been for the best.

The shadows were growing, and the building was only a mass of stucco with some windows lit. Trance music could be heard in the distance. One room in particular called Hack's eye. It had psychedelic lights flickering. It looked as if someone was having a party. Acid churned in the pit of his stomach.

Renton used an infrared gun to look inside the building.

"Many women on the left, two men in the main area, and one woman in the far-right end," the captain informed him.

"We go to the right. That one has to be her." Hack swallowed hard. It was the window with the lights.

"Her readings are off the charts."

"Meaning?"

"We'll see." The man looked worried but didn't say more.

They ran low, hiding as much as possible. The jungle had been cleared and there were a few bushes and trees, but mostly open grass. The first round of fire came when they were fifty feet from the house. It didn't get them, but they knew they had been seen.

Renton went flat to the ground, gave the infrared gun to Hack and pulled out a sniper rifle with silencer that he carried across his back.

He aimed carefully.

Time seemed to stop.

He got a clear shot and hit one of the men.

Hack was watching through the infrared gun.

The second man ran toward the back of the house and simply vanished, or at least his infrared signal did.

Hack assumed he had gone underground. He aimed the gun behind them in a circle and it looked clear from people. Only animals registered, off in the distance.

"We can move," Hack said, getting up and sprinting.

"Did I get our guy?" Renton asked, catching up.

"Don't think so."

They moved fast and low, hiding in the shadows of the trees. They could hear shots over the roar of the fire coming from the jungle. Both men approached the window with the crazy lights and Hack could feel the heavy rhythm of the music in his bones. The window was barred.

"Now what?" he asked Renton.

The man smirked and took out something that looked like a small flashlight. *Where does he hide so much shit?* Renton put on a pair of glasses, clicked a button and the flashlight became a torch. He cut two bars clean through, creating enough space to squeeze inside on their sides.

The place looked like a bachelor pad. Under the fluctuating lights Hack could see the table set with an ugly, toothy fish on it. He rolled his eyes. *Way to go, Romeo.* The room had two doors, one leading to a bedroom, and the other to a long corridor. Just a couple of steps down the hallway door lay Janice, her sundress lifted and masturbating as if her life depended on it. It would have been a hot view were it not evident she was not herself at the moment. Hack promised to kill the bastard who had done this to her, when he got the chance.

He crouched beside her, "Janice," he called.

"Hack?" Her eyes were unfocused. Her irises, huge.

"Let's go home, sweetheart."

"Make love to me. I need you."

"I will, as soon as we are safe. Now we have to leave."

She extended her arms to him, and he picked her up.

Crossing the room again, they went out the window.

Renton was already on the other side and extended his arms to catch her. She squeaked and held onto Hack's neck for dear life.

"It's alright, love. He's with me."

Her arms flew over toward Renton's neck, and he held her while Hack squeezed out through the bars.

"Can you run?" Hack asked Janice.

She answered with a groan.

Renton shook his head.

Hack bent over and picked her up like a potato bag.

"Let's go," he muttered through gritted teeth. It was going to be a long run.

Renton took out night goggles and put them on Hack's forehead above his eyebrows, doing the same with himself. He nodded one time and broke into a light jog.

The shadows had grown impossibly long now, and the last light of the day was dying. It would have been a perfect sunset if it were not for the fact that they were running for their lives.

About a mile ahead, Hack stopped to breathe.

"Hack, it's burning. Can you make it go away?" Janice asked, with tears in her eyes.

"Hold on, baby." Hack looked at Renton. "Anything we can do?"

Renton squinted, assessing her. "If she could walk, it would help."

"I'll do anything," she said, her lower lip quivering.

"Let's go, honey. You can do it."

Hack was furious beyond measure. *He's gonna pay for this.*

Janice took her sandals off and sprinted.

"Take it easy," Renton whispered, catching up with her. "Find a comfortable pace and keep it."

They ran another mile and stopped again. Janice was breathing hard and sweating profusely, Hack touched her arm and her temperature was very high, too high.

"Drink slowly," Hack gave her a bottle with Quinton water.

"Yuck! It's salty," she made a face but drank all of it greedily.

Both men chuckled.

"I know," Hack answered.

"Can I have more?"

"Just a bit later." Quinton water was too salty to drink too much of it at once and Hack was worried she would not hold it.

She gave him the empty bottle back and ran again.

Hack noticed her eyes were more focused. Good.

They heard a noise at their left, and Renton growled: "Down."

Hack tackled Janice and covered her with his body. She had the presence of mind of not to curse too loud.

A battery of silent bullets flew over their heads, scattering pieces of tree bark and leaves.

"Están por aquí," a voice called.

"They are this way," Janice whispered the translation.

"I know. Shut up," Hack murmured in her ear.

Renton looked at him and he nodded. The man slid over his stomach away from them, while Hack squeezed Janice's arm, hoping she would understand and stay quiet.

She had a different idea though. She started moaning. *What the fuck?*

"Sí, así. Mmm..." She breathed, squirming and moaning loudly. *What the fuck?*

"Let me on top," she hissed under her breath. He understood but didn't like it one bit. Yes, they were sitting ducks here, but pretending to be just another couple making love under the moonlight? With his vest and goggles? He tried to roll them out of there, but only managed to get her on top as she wanted. She sat, opened her legs, lifted her dress and started jumping up and down, moaning noisily and massaging her breasts. She was a vision. *Holy shit!*

The woman was crazy. He *would* spank her until his hand hurt for this.

Three men appeared and stopped stunned, watching the show. Before they could take any action, Renton was on them. He cut the first man's throat and kneed the second in the kidney. The same knife that had cut the first man found its way into the third's heart, while a second knife went right to the second kidney of the man on the floor. It was game over before it even started.

Hack was speechless. He'd known the man was good when hiring him but had never seen him in action. Renton was worth every penny of his fat paycheck.

Without stopping, Renton picked up Janice and sprinted, putting her over his shoulder. Hack ran after them.

They were away from the clearing now, and the jungle was getting dense. Night and jungle didn't work together well, not even with night goggles. There were jaguars and snakes. And spiders. Even those stupid tiny red frogs could kill you if you touched them.

Renton stopped to breathe.

"My turn," Hack whispered, and the other man passed Janice to him.

Fuck. He would pay a million bucks for a Jeep right now.

They changed the rhythm to a spirited walk. Running was not the best idea when there were so many obstacles. Renton went first, cutting a path with his knife in the entangled greenery. Hack was right behind him with Janice on his shoulder.

They were both out of breath when they finally reached the river.

Looking into the distance, they realized they were not alone. The men hadn't shaken their tail completely.

They jumped into the boat and turned on the engine.

They heard screams and the unmistakable noise of shotguns being fired. The water around them was splashing.

"Mackey!" Renton roared.

One of the team members aimed a beastly machine gun at the men by the shore and emptied the whole belt.

The attackers ran for cover, giving the rescuers enough time to move out of reach.

Hack had Janice in his arms. She was still sweating profusely. He looked at Renton.

"Here." He passed another water bottle. "Keep her hydrated. And when she starts coming down, don't leave her alone. The feeling of despair is quite strong. Some become suicidal."

The men following them seemed to have given up, and they were alone on the river.

"What did that bastard give her?" asked Hack, hugging her possessively.

"Chemical shit. Looks like a variation of ecstasy."

"Sparkling wine and foul-tasting water," Janice interjected.

"He mixed it with alcohol? That's a big No-no. She could have died. *Asshole*." Renton lost part of his aplomb and shook his head.

"How long does it last?" Hack inquired.

"It depends on the person. For first timers, and a quarter of pill, about half an hour."

Hack noticed the mark of fingers on her face. "The bastard hit you!"

She giggled. "I told him you were my real first. He didn't like it…"

All eyebrows raised, including Hack's. "You did that, hmmm?"

"Yes." The air seemed to have cleared her mind. "And that was not all. I was extremely rude to him. I just…" she glanced down and her eyes filled with tears. She started sobbing uncontrollably. "He said he would kill you, so I had to change his wrath toward me to keep you safe, and… I just exploded. I'm feeling very, very sad now, like if my mom had died."

"Hold on, it'll go away," Renton said.

She nodded and kept on crying.

* * *

Marcos

"Juan, talk to me," Marcos said. *Who the hell are these guys? And what do they want with me?*

"They're at the river, Comandante. They have a boat. Two other men are arriving with a woman. They're carrying her."

"What? Send me pictures. The two men and the woman."

He couldn't believe his eyes. They had Yani.

"Fire on the boat, but don't hurt the woman, or the man who carries her. I want them alive."

"Comandante, they have a machine gun!"

"Get down!"

Marcos heard strangled noises coming from the speaker and knew more of his men had been hit. He cried his frustration and punched the wall with his fist.

"Juan, how many down?"

"Five, sir. Two gone, three might make it."

"Bring them home."

"Yes, Comandante."

"Juan, they went to Mitú or down the river?"

"Down toward Yauareté."

"Thanks."

Marcos cleaned his eyes and smirked. He had them.

He punched some buttons on his phone.

"Aeroporto de Iauareté," a voice answered.

"Marcos here. Do you have a gringo plane there?"

"Yes."

"Don't let them take off. Send the gendarmes and bring them to me."

"Yes, Comandante."

Chapter 31

Hack

"What do you mean we don't have permission to leave?" Hack spat at his pilot.

The man looked at his boss nonchalantly. "Just that, sir. I asked for permission to take off, and the tower didn't give it. We need to wait."

"Wait for what?"

"Another plane to land, paperwork to be issued… Third world countries are a bureaucratic nightmare."

"Take off anyway," Hack ordered.

"Sorry, sir. I can't."

"I understand. Mr. Renton," he called.

"Yes, sir."

"I will be flying the plane out of here against the airport's will and pilot's advice. You and your men are free to choose to stay back with the pilot."

The pilot gawked at him as if he had grown two heads. "They'll send fighters and shoot us down."

"No, they won't." Hack replied, his jaw set.

"I'll fly," Renton quipped. "You watch our six with that computer of yours."

Hack glared at the pilot. "You coming or staying?"

The man shook his head grumpily, shifted to the copilot seat and fastened his belt.

The plane was already on the single runway of the airport, so Renton simply turned on the engines and took off.

The tower yelled at them and threatened to ask for the air force help. They could hear machine gun fire all around them, but nothing vital was hit.

Hack pulled his sat phone.

"Presidência, boa tarde."

"Joao, it's Hack Humphrey."

"Oh, Mr. Humphrey. What a pleasant surprise."

"Is Mr. President around?"

"I'm sorry, he is busy. Video conference."

"Alright. Remember our conversations about opening a local warehouse of H. H. LLC?"

"Yes, of course. We encourage investors to come to Brazil, always. The tax exemptions you asked for though are beyond our ability to oblige."

"I need a favor. If you do this for me, we're signing under your conditions: a forty-million dollar investment to start, and contracting will be ninety percent local. No tax exemptions."

"I'm listening."

"I'm in Iauareté airport, city of Yauareté, and just took off without the tower permission. Can you call the fighters off?"

"What are you doing in the middle of the Amazon?"

"Long story. Can you save my ass? I can't invest if I'm dead."

"On one condition," the man hinted.

"Name it."

"Come straight to Brazilia, I will send word to the fighters to escort you."

"Man, you're a tough negotiator."

"What can I say? I'm from Río."

Hack chuckled. "See you in a couple of hours."

"We'll have the contracts ready."

Hack ended the call and went to the back of the plane to check on Janice, still smiling. Being with this woman had taken the phrase high maintenance to the next level. He'd just lost over sixty million dollars, just for the following five-year period.

He found her sleeping.

Seeing her, with her yellow sundress and her angel face took all calculations of earnings he'd miss out of the equation.

Hack sat on the bed and studied his reflection in the small dresser mirror. He seemed younger; his eyes were bright and the five o'clock shadow gave him a roguish look. He was dirty and sweaty, and happy. Just over two months ago he'd thought he was going down the chute to heart attack and death. He could feel his heart now, beating stronger than ever before. His woman was a miracle.

"Hack?"

"Yes, sweetheart. How are you feeling?"

"Dirty and horny."

"It's probably the remnants of the drug that asshole gave you. It'll go away."

"I don't think so..."

"Hmmm?" He arched his brows.

"Hmmm?" She arched only one.

"Oh, I see... would you like to join the mile-high club?" he asked, sliding a hand up her thigh.

"What's that?" She grinned.

"Let me show you."

* * *

Hack retrieved a plastic bottle and a cloth. He embedded the cloth in water and put both of Yani's feet on his lap. With small circles he started rubbing her feet, cleaning them.

Yani chuckled.

"What?"

"I used to fantasize about you rubbing my feet. I can't believe it's happening."

"Oh yeah? And what else did you fantasize about?"

His hands where now at her ankles, massaging and cleaning. Yani was seriously turned on. She stretched lazily and he kissed the bridge of her foot.

"I used to imagine we made love in the shower…"

"Mmm. Did you come for me then?"

He rubbed knees and thighs, kissing his way up.

"I did. But it was nothing like the real thing."

He smiled wolfishly and urged her to sit, taking the sundress off. His eyes roamed hungrily over her naked body. She felt a pang of anxiety and sucked her stomach in. He chuckled and went on with his methodical cleaning-rubbing-kissing exercise.

By the time his mouth touched hers, Janice was desperate. And Hack was too, if the size of his rod showing through his pants was indication.

"I need you inside…"

"I'm bathed in sweat and mud, sweetheart. It would be like beauty and the beast."

She opened the fly of his cargo pants. "You're a hot-looking beast then, and I want you inside."

With a challenging smile, she mounted him. "Remember the jungle?" She took his shaft in her hands and positioned it, sliding all the way in one try.

Hack grunted and dug his fingers in her hips.

"Woman, you are driving me crazy…"

"I'm just getting started."

She ground her hips and undulated her body in a sinuous dance that was pure sensuality.

"I'm not going to last…"

Yani felt empowered. Liberated. Hack had that effect on her. She felt she could be her boldest self and he would take anything in a stride. Because he was strong enough to handle it, he didn't need to oppress her.

Pressure built in her lower belly and tears welled in her eyes. He felt so right inside her, and he had come all the way to Colombia to rescue her. She let go of the small control she had left. Her hips and her heart ran free.

And she came, screaming her release like a celebration of life, of rebirth.

Hack grunted and let his head fell on the bed. He had been holding it by sheer will, and now he let go, coming with her.

Epilogue

Yani

The waves rolled lazily over the sand and Yani stretched her sun-tanned bikini clad body. She had lost some weight and looked more toned from the miracle of coconut water right from the fruit and long sessions of passionate lovemaking. Hack was beside her with his laptop and a headset, talking to the air in German and moving his hands.

They had spent five days in Brazilia and then flew to Buzios. A short helicopter ride landed them in yet another secluded cove in a beautiful island. They had been here for twenty days already and Hack didn't say when they would go back to New York, but he spent more and more time glued to his toys, so it was coming.

Yani adjusted fast to this life. She almost didn't notice Renton and his men guarding the beach anymore, nor the guys from the Brazilian secret service. Well, those were a bit more notorious because, in contrast with Renton's Spartan pose, they seemed to eat her with their eyes, and they loved to play games.

Janice sheltered her face from the sun and looked at the one that was the closest. The guy was a moreno with shoulder-long hair tied in a ponytail and gym-built torso. He was wearing a sunga and a hat while pretended to sleep under a palm tree. *Where does he have the gun? Better not to ask.* The man smiled, showing a mile of teeth, and winked. She blushed and turned around.

Hack's big paw took her hand possessively.

"Promise me that if you ever need variety you'll talk to me first."

She sat, startled. "What are you talking about?"

He just did a short gesture toward the secret service guy.

Her eyes opened wide.

"Do you really think I would…?"

"Not now. But in ten years… maybe."

"Hack, I wouldn't…"

He crossed his index finger over her mouth. "It's alright, sweetheart. I know I'm lousy company. Not exactly a sensitive guy… or even sensible at times." He grinned and she smiled back, shaking her head in disbelief. "But I do love you. If you ever feel too lonely, or I'm acting like an ass, or anything… you just talk to me first, instead of looking for another guy. Ok?"

"Hack, I wouldn't…" *Did he just say he loves me?*

"Say *ok* then."

She sighed. "Ok. And I won't ever look again. I promise."

"You can look, you can smile… just don't touch."

"You are impossible," she laughed.

"You know it." He took her hand to his lips and kissed her salty fingers. "And that's why you love me?" He said it casually, but there were raw emotions in his face: love, fear, hope.

She smiled and her eyes sparkled with tears. "Yes, I love you because you're impossible. I love you because you're brave. I love you because you're wicked clever. I love you because you're generous. I love you because you're the best lover I've ever had and the only one I want. I love you because you let me be me. I love you because you love me back."

She gave him a small peck on the lips, and her fingers caressed the line of his jaw. He fisted her hair and kissed her deeply, hungrily. She answered the kiss, their lips feasting, their tongues mating.

"Let's go inside," he breathed when they surfaced for air.

Yani nodded. They stood up and walked briskly toward the beach house.

Dear reader,

Thanks for giving this book a try. I hope you had as much fun reading it as I had writing it. And if you didn't, well, I wish you find the books that give you what you are looking for.

If you have comments, suggestions, questions, anything, I would love to hear from you. You can contact me by email at: contact@anadantra.com

Other contact channels:
Publisher pages: https://www.nextchapter.pub/authors/ana-dantra
Website: AnaDantra.com
Facebook: @AnaDantra

See you next time,
♥ Ana ♥

You could also like:
Tango With Me by Ana Dantra

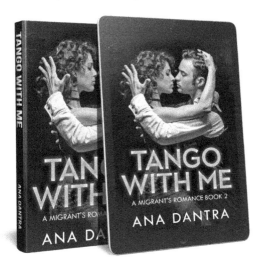

To read the first chapter for free, please head to:
https://www.nextchapter.pub/books/tango-with-me

About the Author

Ana Dantra is a pen name. The woman behind the character is a mom of two teenagers and a cat, who lives somewhere in South America at this time. She lived in Spain for a while and the USA for several years, where she met very interesting people, both local and immigrants. Her stories are all fictitious, but the amazing people she encountered in her travels certainly planted seeds and shaped her views.

A Migrant's Romance Series

Life Hack (Book 1, Colombia)
Tango With Me (Book 2, Argentina)
Dreams of Chuy (Book 3, Uruguay)

Life Hack
ISBN: 978-4-86747-749-6

Published by
Next Chapter
1-60-20 Minami-Otsuka
170-0005 Toshima-Ku, Tokyo
+818035793528
26th May 2021

Lightning Source UK Ltd.
Milton Keynes UK
UKHW011835100621
385314UK00001B/117

9 784867 477496